The characters in this book are entirely fictional. Any resemblance to actual persons living or dead is entirely coincidental. The story is based on true events but changed for dramatic purposes.

She left in the Night

© 2022, V.M. Hill

Self-published

All rights reserved.

No part of this publication may be reproduced, stored in a retrieval system, stored in a database and / or published in any form or by any means, electronic, mechanical, photocopying, recording or otherwise, without the prior written permission of the publisher.

Table of contents

Chapter 1

Maria's job was very tiring. She loved her life, but she was very ambitious and probably worked more than she should. To her, it felt like the years were fleeting away, like she had just graduated from university. But she'll be turning twenty-nine tomorrow. Her student days were long gone. In her early twenties, she loved partying, meeting new people, and just experiencing life. As the years progressed, Maria developed too, and she soon found that life had a broader meaning. To grasp opportunities in the business world, she did her grinding. She had established herself well. When she reached her thirties, she would be well off. She had a job that she loved, many friends, and someone to come home to in the evenings. Her long-time boyfriend—smart, intelligent, and loving—was living with her. His name was Mikael. They were a great team and always supported each other. They tried to put each other first as often as possible. With words and small gestures, they tried to show each other regularly how much they cared about each other. And that's what he did when Maria woke up on Sunday.

Their bedroom was commodious. Their apartment was in the middle of the city. Even though Maria was still in her morning gown and her eyes were still slumberous, her curly hair was bouncing. The moment she entered her living room, her eyes were wide open, and she was fully awake.

Sunday, November 3, 2021.

Standing at the threshold of the living room, she could see a lot of presents. In the middle of the room was a big cake—her favorite: a simple chocolate cake, most likely made from her mother's recipe. She turned around to Mikael, who had already gotten up from their bed and was walking towards her. Clasping her waist and pulling her back, he buried his face in her neck and whispered, "Happy birthday."

She turned her head slightly and softly kissed Mikael. "Thank you, love." she replied. "You always do this. I have to brush my teeth first."

"I don't care," he said. Maria could feel his beard. She then touched his head gently, furling her fingers to feel the silkiness of his hair. "I didn't want to wish you at 12' o'clock, though I quietly did as you were sleeping. I know how cranky you get when someone wakes you in the middle of the night," he said, looking at their dog.

"Aren't you a caring boyfriend?" she said. "I even turned off my phone, so I could get a good night's sleep."

The couple canoodled for a second before Maria stepped into the bathroom, which was beside their bedroom. Everything there was systematic. She entered the shower and turned on the water. She heard a phone buzzing but thought the sound was coming from their neighbour's apartment. Because of the old pipes they had in the building, they could hear everything their neighbours did in their bathroom.

"Maria, your phone. It won't stop," Mikael said.

She was certain she had turned it off last night. Why was it turned on now? Even though the shower could have been longer, a part of her told her to quickly pick up the phone. Not wasting time to dry herself, she rushed out of the bathroom.

Her boyfriend sat in the living room directly across from the bedroom. Cross-legged and sipping his tea, he watched as Maria picked up her phone, thinking it was a call from her office. She realized it wasn't when she saw the many picture notifications that had flooded her phone screen. The look on her face changed as she stared at the phone screen. Mikael, who sat from afar, could tell something was wrong.

"Hey, is everything all right?" he asked.

Maria met his eyes. "Yes, I got a bunch of notifications. Do you remember when I went to Turkey for my birthday?"

Her boyfriend nodded.

"I got a notification of that trip's tagged photos. That was a crazy time."

"But you don't seem too thrilled about it? Is something wrong?" asked Mikael.

Maria sighed and, after a second, said, "I wanted to keep in touch with them because Alissa and Simone, the girls I went on the trip with, had eventually become my friends. They still were when I returned from the trip, but one of them completely disappeared. Perhaps… there is more to it."

"Which one?"

"Alissa," she replied. "We met there for the first time and had a really great weekend. But most of the time, I felt that something was wrong. Back then, I really thought it was a great trip. But when I think back, of all the things that I saw, I feel like I should have been more vigilant. Shortly after the trip, Alissa just disappeared from all social media. She had this Turkish boyfriend. I'm not sure about it, but I think there is more to the story."

Mikael got up and told her that he was going to make them breakfast. He told Maria that till then, she should take her mind off of it and put on the dress he had bought her. It would make her happy. It was cold and dark outside, but Maria was in full agreement with him. When she came out, Maria was in her denim and white tunic. Her outfit gave a sharp enhancement to her persona, especially her dark, bouncing curly hair. The breakfast that her boyfriend had cooked was great. The day went by quickly; they went out for lunch with a few friends. In the evening, both of their families got together for Maria's birthday celebration. Even her family decided to fly in. She caught herself a few times thinking about Alissa and Simone. Where are they right now? She asked herself. What happened to Alissa? Is everything alright? Throughout the day, her emotions were flaring her essence with these thoughts that Maria couldn't answer.

At the end of the day, she was happy with how her birthday had turned out. She took some mindfulness classes but realized that it didn't work today. Her thoughts were all over the place. It mainly included the office work at first, but a large chunk was devoted to Alissa and Simone. She thought her mind would eventually slow down when she went to bed. Even though she had a lot of fun today, she was tired. Maria expected the day's exhaustion to result in a good night's sleep, but it didn't. Mikael fell asleep faster than usual. Hours after they went to bed, Maria was still wide awake. Maria picked up her phone on her nightstand. She then began searching on social media to see if she could find some answers there.

"These are the old photos," she said in a low voice. "Alissa was tagged in the pictures, but the profiles have been deleted."

She checked every picture again, but Alissa was in none of them. As she looked and found nothing, she became increasingly frustrated. She then ended up going through their old emails. The moment she found Alissa's email address, she sent her a message that simply said, "Hey Alissa… was thinking of you. How are you doing?" A few seconds after sending it, a notification popped up on her phone. She had received an email! Full of excitement, she opened her email only to read:

The recipient has been deleted or has no e-mail address.

It meant that Alissa's email didn't exist anymore. Maria got really frustrated. She opened her social media account and then ended up checking Simone's profile through the photo she was tagged in. Judging by her profile picture, she was doing well for herself. Simone looked nothing like she did in her late thirties. She looked great. She had gained a small fan base over the years. Maria was not surprised; Simone worked hard on her appearance. In 2016, Simone was in her late twenties and Alissa was twenty. She looked like a model. It matched her long nails and long eyelashes. Both Alissa and Simone were very similar when it came to their looks. They both had long blonde hair, looked very sporty, had long eyelashes and long nails.

Maria decided to reach out to Simone. She had little hope that Simone would answer, considering that she had gained several thousand followers over the years. "Hey! I can't believe it's you!" she said.

"I feel the same. It's been a while," Maria wrote. They then ended up asking what was happening in their lives after five years. Maria then, at last, asked, "Do you know what is up with Alissa?"

"Not since the last time we met," she texted back.

"That was a long time ago. Anything you know about her currently?"

"No, I don't know," Simone replied, "I'm curious as well. She was such a lovely girl."

"I couldn't agree more."

"I often go to Side on vacation, but usually with my family. I haven't heard from Alissa since 2016, I think."

Maria started to think about Alissa's boyfriend. His name was Adem. A very corny guy with a cynical sense of viewing things. That's how she had perceived him the first time she had seen him. He was wearing a suit. He appeared fancier than anything he could afford. Besides, to link everything back to Alissa, her life seemed to have many twists and turns. From living in Germany to ending up in Turkey with Adem, there were a plethora of factors involved that could lead to bad outcomes. All the "what if's" that came to her mind bugged her. She was usually a rather optimistic person, but given the circumstances, she had a bad feeling.

She knew Alissa's relationship was tainted by jealousy and power. Thinking more about it, she began to worry. Maria had a spontaneous side, which had remained consistent over the years. And this side overcame her that night. She logged out of her social media accounts and booked a flight to Turkey.

Taking that step made her calm down. She eventually became so calm that she managed to fall asleep. When she woke up, she told Mikael right away. He was baffled. He couldn't understand his girlfriend's rush decision.

"What are you trying to do?" he exclaimed.

"I'm worried about Alissa. I can't find her anywhere," Maria replied.

"Maybe she's just staying off social media?"

"Maybe," she answered. "But so many things just don't add up. I remember that a few months after we met, she posted so many pictures of her and Adem, only to delete them shortly after. It just doesn't make sense. And if you had seen them together, you would be worried too."

"You sound like Jason Bourne," he said. "Don't you think you're acting rashly? If Alissa is in danger, don't you think you'll be putting yourself in danger as well? What about your safety? Did you think about that? I'm not badgering you, because I support you. I'm just asking you to be pragmatic. I wouldn't have mind if you had explained to me what was on your mind. I was wondering what had gotten into you on your birthday."

"I know. You are right. But I just had this feeling. I have to do it. And I'm sorry you tried so hard to make sure I had the best day. I was a bit off on my birthday. Mikael, I know you have a hard time understanding, but the truth is, I couldn't resist. I just need to know what happened to Alissa. It all started with that stupid notification."

Mikael was almost out the door; he was already a little late for work. But he was worried for his girlfriend more than Maria was worried for Alissa. What if something happens to her? Traveling alone can be dangerous for a young woman. What if…He couldn't get rid of all the what-ifs. The biggest one included the stories that Maria had told him about what happened six years ago. Those stories with his girlfriend, Alissa, and Simone weren't that great in terms of safety, even though a part of him had once found the stories intriguing. But not now, especially when it could result in serious ramifications.

"Do you want me to stay?" asked Maria. "I'm asking you directly."

Mikael looked at her for a second and then asked, "What does it matter? I can't stop you. We both know that."

"If you want me to stay, I'll stay," Maria answered.

He exhaled loudly, kissed Maria and left.

Chapter 2

At first, one would think Antalya was like Miami. The only difference would be that one was in the United States and the other one was in Turkey. But Antalya was more famous for its tourist attractions. Commonly, the peak of any tourist spot would include beaches and, perhaps, mountains. But Antalya had a dense historic significance that also included natural wonders. Besides, the summers were long. The beaches would thrive. From Lara Public Beach to Cleopatra Beach, the ones who didn't want to walk too far away from their hotels to attend such beaches resided in Side.

It was a district in Antalya. That's what Simone was talking about: that she visited this place four times per year, but nothing was found when it came to Alissa. But when it came to good hotels, good cafes, and some restaurants, Side was the place. And that was the place that Maria had in mind before taking the airplane. The objective was the Palm World Side

Resort & Spa. In 2016, that hotel was where she, Alissa, and Simone resided. Now, Maria had to go alone.

Meanwhile, Mikeal had also informed her about the place as he had also done some research. "It looks safe," he said, "but still, it looks like the whole world goes there, so you have to be careful. On the other hand, I have to admit, I have never seen such a beautiful place. I guess that's what ten different civilizations thought when they discovered Antalya."

He was trying to lighten his girlfriend's mood. She did feel cheered up a bit when he continued speaking, "Go, and find me a heaven on earth.' This was what King Attalos of Pergamon said to his men before they discovered Antalya. Then there were Lydian times, followed by Byzantine, and then Seljuk, and the last was the Ottoman Empires. You really went to a good place that turned out bad. Perhaps it was bad from the start. You just didn't know it."

That's what Maria was thinking when she was finally aboard the plane. It felt like a mission to her, but it was a mission with no plan, even if her boyfriend had done some briefing. Mikael was supportive; Maria was now certain, though she had always known. She felt so clueless and stupid as she sat on the plane. In the movies, this part always looked so simple.

It was more than a few hours' journey. Maria was curious most of the time. Her heart was beating fast. Nothing made sense. And although Maria tried to make sense of her situation, it wasn't that easy.

Unable to sit in one place, which happened a few times as the flight took a bit of an hour, Maria would go to the bathroom to pass her time. Even if she didn't have to use the loo, she would look at herself in the mirror. Her black dress complemented her curly hair and brown eyes. She looked calm and content, but that was not how she felt on the inside. She liked experiencing things outside of her comfort zone, but this felt different. At that moment, she even missed her office.

"You don't know what you are doing. The only thing you booked is the hotel and a driver?" She thought to herself as she looked in the mirror. Her thoughts were interrupted by the sudden announcement made by the stewardess, advising the passengers to return to their seats.

When she returned to her seat, she realized that they were almost at Antalya International Airport. From her window seat, she could see a projection of a deep blue sea. The Taurus mountains, which were hidden in bays and coves, surrounded them. They flew by quickly as another mountain came into view below them. It was as if parts of turrets were spread, but in actuality, they looked like cottages with red sheds and blue sky. Soon after, they landed.

There were big letters that spelt 'WELCOME TO' in blue and 'ANTALYA' in almost orange. The airport was like a mall with a white marble floor and the ceiling was like when you go out for a game and then during the break time, you go to take a snack at the back. That was the feeling inside the airport. But Maria was feeling strange as she took the elevator. There wasn't that much of a crowd. Covid restrictions protocols were observed. The eating stalls were almost shut except for two or three cafes inside. But Maria's aim was to go outside as she stood in Terminal 2. She felt a bit of relief as the driver she had booked in advance was already holding a sign with her name written on it.

"Hey," she said, extending her hand out to him.

The gray-haired man nodded at her and that was all. The taxi outside the airport was normal looking. Even though there were fewer people around, Antalya was beautiful from the moment she sat inside the taxi on her way to Palm World Side Resort and Spa. The location wasn't exactly in Side, the ancient city, but a few kilometers away from that place where Side Road, which was also known as Side Street, began.

The journey was somehow long. It almost took another hour to reach the resort that Maria once visited. On the way, she saw the beaches. The same with mountains and different industrialized coastal areas that she couldn't recognize. Only the memories of late-night parties from the last time she was here lingered in her mind. Aside from that, she remembered how that particular morning was inside the hotel, not outside.

She thought about whether she would be able to meet the people she once met and whether they would know the whereabouts of her friend, Alissa. Well, that felt like a mission. And when Maria thought of her objective in that term, Side

Road came into view. She could see all the palm trees on each side.

The resort looked the same but with fewer crowds. The blue swimming pool that stood on the façade was the center of attraction. The building wasn't that high in height, but it was quite broad in width. Most of its white color matched the blue shades of the railings. That was the general décor of the resort with everything. Whether it was the bedrooms or halls, white and blue dwelled in patterns. It also complimented the environment outside, mostly the beach.

The rest of the area was covered by some small structures. Around the swimming pool was space for at least a hundred sunbeds, and the ground floor not only covered the main resort but also the corners of the areas where the entire resort stood. This was where various sections, mainly restaurants and spas, were located.

Maria had reached her destination, but she was still clueless and tired. Before she could go to her room, she decided to sit in the main hall. This was where she had sat the last time with Alissa, who felt under the control of Adem, her boyfriend. The previous incident of the night that Maria had with her was also weird. Yet she couldn't forget about it because that night was when she had seen Alissa for the last time.

"Is the bar open?" That was her first question when she walked over to the receptionist.

"Yes," the receptionist had answered, "but you will hardly find anybody there."

Maria nodded and headed in that direction. It didn't feel like part of the resort, but it was. The ceilings were rainbow-colored. The counter was stocked with different drinks, and the music playing in the club was low and dull.

Sitting at the counter, Maria asked herself, "Now what?"

Things felt thrilling as she boarded the plane. But now she felt bored and a little bit scared because some part of her felt that she was in a beautiful but unknown land. Even though it was a tourist attraction, one had to keep their eyes open no matter what. It didn't matter if she had been there before.

"Is Engin still here?" she asked the bartender.

"He quit three years ago," he replied.

Engin was the man that once served the three of them. Maria decided to check different places on the ground floor to see if she would meet any of the people who worked at this resort when she and the girls were here in 2016. Maria didn't know them all because she had a vague memory of them, but still, she had to give her full effort. To find Alissa, all she had was her photo that she, Alissa, and Simone were tagged in. Other than that, she had nothing. It was hard and a thought inside of her lingered that made her ask, "Why didn't I take more photos?"

To answer that question, she tried to remind herself of why she was there. It was surely an experience and fun at first. The most prominent were linked to Alissa and Adem. As far as the party was concerned, it didn't live up to the hype. The only excitement was when the three girls were leaving their countries and when they came to reside at this resort.

From the bar, Maria then headed to one of the restaurants that was inside, not opened and close to the pool. She was looking for Selim. At least, that was the name written on his badge when he came to serve her breakfast the last time before she left. Instead, another waiter appeared to serve her a mint drink. She turned to him and asked, "Do you know anybody by the name of Selim?"

"May I ask his last name because there are a few Selims working here," he replied.

Maria didn't know his last name, so she decided to call it a day. She was already tired. She had expected to run into some of the people she had interacted with the last time, show them Alissa's picture, and then inquire about her whereabouts. But as soon as she went to her room, that felt like a flop plan.

"I'm tired as hell," she said as she tossed her purse on the bed.

She clearly wasn't Sherlock Holmes and, so far, nothing was making her feel like there was hope. Something inside of her told her to move on. "But how?" she thought to herself. "To first get some rest." The afternoon was winding down and the evening was approaching. When Maria looked out her window, she could see different side streets and the gloomy sky above them—gloomy, like her state of mind. The same with the streets, whose lanes were in a labyrinth. The accumulated strain, combined with her jet lag, made her feel as if the strength in her body was gone and her emotions had vanished the second she lay on the bed. She had no control over the situation and no clue on how to find Alissa.

When she finally woke up, it was late in the evening. Before changing her clothes, she called her boyfriend. "Yes, I'm fine, Mikael," she said.

"I called you so many times," he spoke. "I was so worried. At least, answer my messages."

"I did," she said, and removed the phone from her ear to confirm, only to find that the message hadn't been sent yet.

"When?"

"Never mind," she replied. "I'm sorry. I was very tired."

"Are you alright?"

"Yes," she said.

"How's the place?"

"Not that much crowd, Mikael. But I think I would now go to the main street to find that optician."

"That jerk—"

"Yes," she interrupted, "he is the closest link to Alissa right now. Deniz might help us even though we can't trust him."

Mikael was typing as he was working. But in his mind, he was thinking about why he had sent his girlfriend there. He was worried. Yet the reality was that, right now, he could just support her decisions. "Take care and be vigilant. If anything comes up, call me."

The evening soon became a bit dark. Even during the restrictions, there were people. Again, taking the cab and finding herself in the main town of Side, there were different streets surrounded by red stalls of food. Most of them were closed, so were some stores as well. Still, some tourists were on the path to explore what this town had to offer in terms of a medieval feel.

All the stores seemed to blend together. The only distinction was their sheds and whether there were any flower trees ready to complement the town. The main street was where the usual rush had occurred, but in 2021, that rush had been greatly reduced. There were many geopolitical reasons, but the one that stood out the most was the pandemic. Though many countries were open now, there was still a hesitation.

Maria's hesitation was to find that optician's store. It was also located near the main street, and everything there felt similar. She was confused, and for some, reason, she felt someone was watching her, which made her stop a few times to look around. That was weird, but it was her insecurity. She was usually the one who enjoyed walking. But that was not the case right, as she had already bumped around in many streets with various yet similar stores and some food stalls, but no sign of any optician.

"Where the hell is he?" she asked herself.

Side was also known for its nightlife, but at that moment, that nightlife didn't feel that promising. It felt like a sensation, but without a goal. A place where the heart wanted to go, but the mind had other plans. Checking the street for a moment, she finally entered a mini-lane that felt familiar, but Maria knew she could be wrong. Almost at its end, there was indeed a store, but it was closed. The store's name was displayed above its extended shed that read, "Dina Optik".

"Was this Deniz's store?" Maria didn't know. Yet it was clear that it was an optician's store.

"What a weird place," she sighed.

Maria's heart was racing. When she turned around, there was a black cat in the middle of the lane. At that, she almost screamed, making a squeal sound. Maria wasn't proud of that; her reaction made it clear that she was not good at roaming the streets alone at night.

Before it could get darker, she decided to return to the resort. After having a dinner that consisted of some local stuffed bread and fruits, Maria retired for the day. This time, she showed the picture to the other bartenders in Palm World Side, but nobody recognized Alissa. One time, she even went to the kitchen to meet another Selim, who once was a waiter.

"Do you recognize her?" Maria asked.

"I don't even recognize you," he had answered in Turkish, which Maria had interpreted using her mobile. Finding Alissa wasn't like in the movies. It wasn't thrilling, either. It was boring while the energy of Maria's body drained her and told her: why are you doing this, Maria? Just go home and forget about everything.

As the hours went by, her energy levels kept on sinking. Meanwhile, the weekend was coming to an end while Maria followed the same drills of roaming the streets and roaming the resort, yet no real progress was made. It made her feel disappointed. The lack of results shook her confidence. The only good thing about this journey was Mikael's texts. He tried to support her.

Also, it turned out that Mikael was in Karain Cave, a place in the north of Antalya that was inhabited for twenty-five thousand years by different civilizations. It was the oldest settlement in Turkey and had the biggest museum in Antalya. She would have gone to that place if she felt like she deserved it.

She couldn't hope but show. She couldn't think but prove. Both of those things weren't happening as her last days in Antalya approached. She felt like a tourist who wanted to enjoy everything but didn't understand the significance of the place. That was Antalya for her—where most stores were closed and what she had set out to do had not been achieved.

She packed her belongings and left her hotel room, ready to leave. At the front desk, she saw a man who was not dressed like the other receptionists and decided to try her luck. "Do you recognize this girl?" Maria asked.

"What's her name?" he answered.

"Alissa," Maria replied.

The man sighed and explained to Maria that many people with such names come to their resort from all over the world, but as the general manager, he is seldom in contact with the guests, unless a problem occurs. She could tell by the look on his face that he really wanted to help her but couldn't. At least that's what she thought. But sadly, there was just one picture of Alissa with her. Nothing else. Maria still couldn't believe that her digital presence was wiped away.

Before leaving Antalya with no result, she again remembered how cheerful Alissa was. It felt strange that she could have so many fans and followers, but she did not exist online. She knew that wasn't the end of her journey. That's what Maria told herself.

Chapter 3

There wasn't much progress in Maria's life. She slept, ate, went to work, went to the university, had dinner, and went to bed. This schedule was monotonous. On the weekends, she would go out with her friends to unwind and forget about the dull week she had had. University life wasn't making sense to her anymore. She expected psychology to be an exciting course, but it was just draining her. Maria didn't have a boyfriend at the time. She had her heart recently broken. Every now and then, she would meet up with a guy who had feelings for her, which she didn't quite understand because they had nothing in common. She would use him to feel better about herself and her life.

At the time, she was twenty-three years old. Her friends would describe her as tall and slim. Her hair was long and curly—which was now a bit damaged as she had been dying it over the past few years. She had dark, chestnut-coloured eyes, which paved the way for people to approach her. Maria was naturally confident, despite the fact that her studies were taking a toll on her. She lived in a newly renovated dormitory with some friends who always had her back.

Every day, she would get up and attend the lectures or go to work. That felt like a scripted life. Although her parents supported her, she still felt the need to be independent. She had already done her minor in psychology. Things were interesting at that time. Now, they were taking another arc that Maria wasn't ready for. There were many assignments; some of which she excelled at and others at which she failed miserably. Also, there were some topics where she helped people. And it was the people in general that made her choose this subject because she was very good with them when it came to talking and trusting, but pursuing that actual profession had made her a bit slouched.

The whole year was tough for her. She moved back home after a bad breakup, but realized she had to move out quickly again. When she moved back into the dormitory, she drank more and partied more than before—it was just so easy. There was always someone up for a drink. Plus, a nightclub was just around the corner. Her parents lived in the same city, but almost in the countryside, so there was not much action there.

They lived an hour away from her. The university was in a different place, so Maria hardly visited them. It wasn't as frequent as it should be. She always used the distance as an excuse, but deep down, she knew that she was all over the place. Her studies were going well, at least to her, but her parents didn't seem to think so. The part-time job in a library wasn't fulfilling. And when she returned home for even one night, her family did nothing but ask her questions.

The reason why she didn't visit them so often was simple: they always discussed the same thing—her life choices, which they sometimes argued about. She always had to defend herself, which was exhausting.

As it was the last year, companies had started to arrive at the universities to select the candidates, but it wasn't for Maria's field. Various companies had different schedules for different fields. All Maria cared about were the holidays. Her birthday was coming up—November 3. She was anxious about it.

Before her twin sister moved, she looked forward to her birthdays and the birthday parties because she knew that, at the very least, people would show up for her sister. Things were a little different now. Maria was well liked, but celebrating her birthday always put an unusual strain on her.

She shared the dormitory with two other girls—Nancy and Jessica. They were the studious ones, but they too had their fun. One was in a long-distance relationship, while the other one had an on-and-off fling going on. It was only Maria who didn't have someone. She thought when it had to happen, it would happen. Although they were with her most of the time, they were occasionally absent since both of them had boyfriends. Maria only joined them when it came to the party and sometimes studying, even though their programs differed. All the girls supported each other like best friends, but they were both gone now, and Maria had arrived from her home quite early.

October 31, 2016.

Maria was sitting in her chair, slouching. Her arms were resting on her knees and she was observing the room that had yellow illumination. Slowly, hopelessness began to beckon her. It was then she said to herself, "I can't let this happen. There must be a solution to my situation. There must be something I can do."

A beautiful scene started forming in her mind when she stood up and stood near the windowsill. The scenery wasn't of her university, but a thought that told her to just go away from this industrialized life that she was indulging in. Quickly, Maria checked her phone and began typing things like '10 beautiful places to visit', 'Budget-friendly places', and 'Places where one can have fun.' With these searches, a lot of travel sites begun to pop up. She contacted some friends, but no one seemed to be available for a get-away together. Many places had her budget, but after a few more Google searches, she found out that there was a group called Plan Together that had a lot of reviews. It made Maria trust that site.

The purpose of that site was to connect people with similar budgets so that they could visit their chosen location. Maria's heart had begun to thump as she logged into the site and entered her details.

"Should I do this?" she asked herself.

The answer was yes because her birthday was in three days. The second she got connected with a girl named Alissa, she was quick to point out, "If you want to have some fun, then Antalya is the place. It's like heaven on earth."

Those words felt beautiful at first, but Maria asked, "How do you know it's my birthday?"

"The site indicates if somebody's birthday is near. The second I got connected, I was notified of it."

"So, we are the only ones who would make this trip?" asked Maria while she was looking at Alissa's profile picture on the site. She looked as if she was a model, but so did many people on their social media, yet Maria was ready to give the benefit of the doubt until proven otherwise.

"Let me see if I can get another person," said Alissa. After two minutes, she came back, and suddenly, a video call was dialed by her. When she answered the call, three windows popped up. Maria was the only one who had dark curly hair. The rest were all blondes. Alissa and Simone felt like sisters. Alissa was the younger one; Simone was the eldest. Both were attractive and seemed friendly.

"I can't wait for your birthday the second I see the notification," said Simone.

"Thank you," said Maria, "but where are we going?"

"Side. Close to Antalya, in Turkey."

Just moments after, the trip was booked. The next couple of days were spent in excitement. Maria was so excited that she would sleep late and wake up early. A day before the trip, she packed her backpack. Finally, there was salvation, she thought. Finally, there was something new in this boring life. A few days of sunshine, cocktails, and fun would elevate her spirit. That was all she could think of.

When her birthday arrived, these girls were the first ones to wish her. It was weird because Maria had known them for just a few days and they were acting as if they had known each other forever. She loved that kind gesture nonetheless.

She left her campus and hailed a cab to the airport. Although it was a beautiful day and Friday had arrived faster than expected, the traffic seemed insane. They highways had been congested, with cars honking incessantly. The boarding was at 12:30 p.m. Though Maria had left her campus early, there was no guarantee that she would get there on time.

"Do you think we will reach the airport…like ever?" she asked the driver.

He chuckled and answered, "Ma'am, I'm trying my best."

A bridge soon passed over the highway. It was built for trains, and when she saw one pass by, Maria wished she could hop on it as it was almost 12 p.m. She told the driver to end their journey so she could board one of the trains. Maria silently thanked herself for only taking one backpack and not too many clothes.

It was 12:09 p.m. when she got to the station. Unfortunately for her, the 12 p.m. first train left just as she arrived. She was nervous and excited as she boarded the second train. She hadn't felt this much excitement in her last three years post-graduation as she was feeling at the moment. Everyone could tell she was nervous, but Maria didn't care. She had Turkey on her mind; she couldn't get the pictures of Antalya that she had seen on the internet out of her head.

The train ride was just a few minutes long, but it felt like an eternity. In her mind, she created a map of the fastest route from the station to her gate. She dashed off of the train when the doors opened. At exactly 12:35, she boarded the plane. She was late, but it hadn't taken off yet, which she was grateful for. After settling down in her seat, she checked her mobile again and texted Alissa that she was finally on her flight. Alissa replied her text, saying she was excited and that she couldn't wait to meet her.

Maria could now finally take a sigh of relief while sitting comfortably in her seat. Plus, now she felt rewarded by the golden rays of the sun dimming down on the horizon. The rest of the earth was surrounded by the sea, and Maria was near the clouds. As it was November, the sun set early. Witnessing the sunset, that feeling felt special until she leaned back against the seat and drifted off to sleep.

When she arrived at Antalya International Airport, it was pretty much empty. She couldn't understand the reason behind it. Plus, there was additional security and soon it was clear that the President of the United States had arrived to visit the country. Due to this, Maria had to go through many security checks, but as she left the airport, she was able to find the taxi.

"Palm World Side," she said, and the driver immediately recognized Maria's destination.

During the evening, the roads felt pretty empty. She opened her window a little bit. First she smelled it, and then she could hear it: the ocean. The sound of the waves hitting the shore wasn't a lot, but it was enough to echo inside of her. That experience was strange. She has seen the coast many times, but this felt different. Besides, the driver wasn't talking that much, which was fine with her. He looked like he was concentrating, and after a short time, they reached their destination.

The Palm World Beach resort was spread over a property whose boundaries were secured by many trees and flowers. The hotel was on the main street in Side.

At the entrance of the resort, stood two beautiful girls. It was obvious who they were. Behind them was the resort. It also had the shine of a hotel, as it had one while it looked quite grand. That feeling made Maria happy, and when she came out of her taxi, she finally met Alissa and Simone in person.

Both were very nice and warmly welcomed her. "I hope the journey was good," said Alissa.

"It was," replied Maria. "There are not that many people around."

"Don't worry," said Simone. "You will meet many people here."

She wasn't happy as the three of them became quadruple and the fourth person wasn't a girl. Instead, it was a man who Maria shook hands with. His name was Adem. He was introduced to her as Alissa's boyfriend. He was her age, and his build was almost slender. Maria didn't get good vibes from him at one of the restaurants in the resort where Alissa had a birthday surprise for her.

She and Simone had set a table with sparkling wine and a great dinner. Turkish cuisine was served, which included all kinds of bread that looked like slices of pizza and desserts that felt like regular cakes. But it was a different flavor, and it was something new for Maria. Meanwhile, Adem kept on observing each one of them as if he was their bodyguard. Maria was all smiles since she was enjoying her birthday, but didn't like that man sitting across from her.

"How did you two meet?" She slipped in that question during their conversation as Adem wasn't talking that much and, through his gestures, pointed out whenever Alissa became too frank.

"We met in Germany," replied Alissa, who was munching on a fruit. "Adem used to work there until he had a visa problem. He had to go back to Turkey. We love each other, so breaking up was not an option. I wanted to move with him to Turkey. It made my visit—" he showed his hand to stop her talking.

"That's… enough," he said in his broken English and uttered something in Turkish. He made an impression, as if that story was embarrassing him, but Maria couldn't understand why.

He insisted on ordering the food and drinks for the girls, as Alissa was not really allowed to talk to other men. Besides, Simone had begun her own story where she told everybody that this wasn't the first time she was visiting Antalya. Maria thought that was good because she needed people around her that were familiar with the place she was in.

The dinner started with wine and ended with champagne. Overall, the dinner was lovely, as was Maria's birthday celebration. As the resort had a few restaurants, they were sitting near the one where they could see the main swimming pool. That was like the center of attraction for Palm World Side. People on the corners were enjoying themselves. Some were swimming during the night. The same atmosphere was in the restaurant, but the time had come for the trio of girls to finally go to the clubs and have some fun.

The resort had a nightclub as well, but Alissa pointed out that Side was a nice area where there were many good clubs, much better than the place they were staying in. Maria had agreed to it. Simone looked as if she knew everything. Was that a good sign? Maria just went along. Also, Adem's car was parked just outside the resort.

Suddenly, they all found themselves leaving the resort. There weren't many people outside until the car slowly headed down the main street of Side. On the way, Maria caught a sight of the beach clearly. Unlike how she felt, the ocean's surface was calm. All she could think about was partying hard.

In the car, Maria learned that Alissa could speak a bit of Turkish as well.

"I think we shouldn't go straight to the club," said Simone, who was sitting beside Maria.

She was very cordial and relaxed about everything, as if she knew the nature of the world and had accepted that nature very well.

"Where should we go?" asked Alissa.

"I have an acquaintance on the main street. His name is Deniz. He is an optician. We should go there. He usually has good drinks in his shop."

"An optician who drinks?" Maria chuckled.

"He is like that," replied Simone. "A bit goofy but a good guy."

Maria became hesitant and conscious of her surroundings as the many streets of Side began to envelop her. Even though she felt a sense of belonging, she wasn't completely at ease. She couldn't understand her emotions. Besides, Adem had pressed the acceleration paddle. From his side, it felt like a reckless sense of ease, as if he was proclaiming that he was the owner of his car and he had now decided to do whatever he wanted to do with it.

The strands of Maria's hair swung as they were making a desperate protest to slow down the car, but when Simone started to enjoy the speed, somehow Maria too got involved in it. The moment the car stopped, Adem turned to Alissa and said, with an accent, "Low petrol," and then glanced at Simone and Maria together.

"Don't worry," replied Simone. "Deniz has his car. We can all fit in."

Adem had parked his car randomly—that is, improperly—near the street's threshold in the center of the Side that paved the way for the main street. There were many conglomerations of things that were on display. It was dark, and most of the stores were closed. Outside the bars, though, there were queues. It gave the impression that there were a lot of people, but if one looked closely, there weren't that many tourists; mostly locals.

As they passed, with Simone leading the way, some stares came in their direction. Adem didn't like that and made sure that Alissa was beside him. Her gesture felt as though she couldn't disapprove; she couldn't stand up for herself or reject his decision. It was strange for Maria to see their relationship. Some local people approached them. One of them was trying to sell bracelets to Maria as they were walking about.

"Ignore them," said Simone.

Maria was looking at Alissa. She kept on being funny so that Maria could feel comfortable. Maria still hadn't gotten used to the fact that Adem was with them. She was sold on the idea of the trio—she, Alissa, and Simone—partying all night without any interruption. But it was still better than dwelling on the campus of the university.

They switched lanes many times during their walk. Maria had her eyes on everything while also trying to enjoy herself.

"The bars here are too crowded and very expensive," said Alissa.

"Deniz knows his way around here," Simone said. "We will have fun tonight. Your birthday is just starting, Maria. "

As the end of the main street came into sight, another smaller street came into view. It wasn't the main street, but the way to the optician's store was in sight. There weren't any walls where too many flowers from the trees were dangling, as this seemed like a decorating habit throughout the Side.

At the end of the street, Maria saw a man. He had a drink in one hand while closing the shutters of a store with the other. When he felt there was a presence nearby, he turned to face the group.

His presence wasn't enlightening. Deniz was already drunk when he joined the group. Even though he was hugging

Simone, his gaze was drawn to Maria first. He then shook hands with Adem and Alissa. When he stood near Maria and shook her hand, he went for the kiss on it. Though Maria tried to maintain her distance, she could still smell his drunken breath. Deniz was acting like he was in a movie, but his presence was just uncomfortable.

Alissa was trying her best to keep everyone in the conversation loop. But Deniz was trying to act superlative while still trying to appear as a rational and likable guy, which he wasn't. There was subtle shading in the way he stood and expressed his intentions, not through words but actions.

As Adem's car was closer to the ground, they all ended up in Deniz's car. It looked big from the outside, but the inside was the same as Adem's car. Maria was sitting beside Simone, and beside her was Alissa. The men sat in the front. Deniz was drinking as if he didn't care about the world. On top of that, he was driving fast. Their destination was now his home because he wanted to change quickly before they hit the club. Maria thought it would make no difference to his persona.

"There is the beach that we will visit tomorrow," said Simone, pointing towards the endless black sea.

"Usually, Side beaches are clean and the ocean is quite wavy. There are also historical sites nearby. We can go sightseeing if we get up early, and we would definitely be able to see the sunset," Alissa said, and laughed.

When the car stopped, Deniz was quick to get out. Meanwhile, Simone kept on talking, saying, "As I said, I have been here before, but the truth is I have been here quite a few times."

"That's why," said Maria.

"That's why what?"

"You were walking as if you knew the place well."

Simone nodded, and at that moment, Deniz came out, wearing something sparkly. He didn't appear to be dressed for a club. His outfit looked like something you would wear for some private occasion. Still, it wasn't good. It evoked neither approval nor delight in Maria. Then finally, they went to a club. It had a rock theme. People were dancing. Everyone was having fun.

The club felt quite dark. It had psychedelic lights all over the ceiling, and the disco ball was pointing its polka dots at everyone's faces. Deniz was the one who had selected the club. On the way, it looked as if Adem knew Deniz. Both spoke as if it wasn't the first time they were conversing. Also, Deniz was leading them to a separate and private counter. Yet it wasn't empty. Two people were sitting there. One of them was a girl. She was a local girl who uttered broken English.

"Lovely… meeting… you guys," she said, as if she was skipping words. Her name was Aisha, and her glance was different when she looked at the person sitting next to her. His name was Ahmet. There was a personal and insolent quality to his smile. Among the two men, he looked quite fit but unhealthy in terms of his manners. His nice behavior appeared forced. If Deniz was an average looking guy in essence to his intellectual capabilities, Ahmet seemed calm, an indication as to whether there was more to the night than Maria, Alissa, and Simone could have imagined.

To Maria, something didn't feel right. This was what her intuition told her. Even while she wanted to just relax and enjoy the evening, she sensed something was crumbling heavily among the new group that she couldn't quite put her fingers on. The vibe of her overall birthday didn't feel right. Except for the dinner, she couldn't tell whether her birthday was worth it or not. For that, there was passive frustration. She was in a different country, and somehow, the motion of time felt different there. It was like an oppressive weight that she wanted to shrug off and just be with the trio. Besides, Maria was eloquent with her voice whenever she had to converse. That was the course of her struggle. Still, she thought it was better than her university. Also, a huge party still awaited her. That's what she thought and tried to counter the instincts that made her feel something was wrong. But the night wasn't over yet, and there was more to come.

Chapter 4

When Maria returned home from Side, many questions were bugging her on the flight. The biggest of them all was still: where was Alissa? It was hard for her to believe that she hadn't found anything about her. It made her hopeless. Despite all that happened there, she had so many good memories of Side. But now, it had become a place where nothing felt fulfilled. Even the first time that she visited the place, nothing was amazing about it, even though that was the perception at first. Maria returned to her country feeling like no chance had been taken and the battle was unfought.

She spotted Mikael at the airport and went to hug him. However, none of them said much on the drive home. Mikael drove, knowing that his girlfriend hadn't found anything, and Maria sat in the passenger seat, staring out the window. The sun had not yet gone down. The evening was still deceptively blue until it slowly started to turn darker, blending into the invisible clouds that her airplane might have touched a few hours ago. These were the clouds that ended up hiding the sun and bringing the night.

Maria was tired when she entered her apartment. She felt like a failure. "Life wasn't a Jason Bourne movie after all," Mikael pointed out. "I told you to find something you really want. You need to do more digging."

"But you never even asked me whether I found something or not," replied Maria.

"I saw your face. It was all the answer I needed," he answered.

Mikael ended up telling her that when one was on a mission, one had to be objective. Getting lost in emotions and acting on those emotions didn't always result in an optimum outcome. Calculating moves was important, and so was understanding the truth. He told Maria that when one counts possibilities, one considers many scenarios. "The truth can sometimes be bittersweet because that's the nature of truth. You have to deal with it, but at the same time, you have to focus on being optimistic too. Why? Because getting lost in negativity is easy and not focusing on the positive side at that moment becomes 'double negative'," he said.

Despite his rational nature, Mikael talked for quite a while. For him, Maria's going to another country was a sudden and major decision by her that he hadn't anticipated. On the other hand, he knew his girlfriend's habits. He knew if Maria was faced with any challenge, she always wanted to resolve the matter quickly. Procrastination wasn't on her radar, and neither was her comfort zone. Always out of it, that was how Maria changed her life after college had ended. Yet a thread of her memory that was once bound to her early twenties had come back. It was her birthday, and it was a party weekend in Side. She has now visited that place twice.

After Mikael was done briefing Maria's situation to her—as if she didn't know already—he went to bed. His girlfriend told him that she would join him later because she had to do some digging. Mikael thought he had motivated Maria enough, and that was true because what her boyfriend was talking about was sensible. He was using his logical faculties even though he was overthinking, whereas Maria was carried away by her spontaneous ideas. They were like the clots of mist in front of the moon that could be seen outside her balcony. The mist was drifting and was making the moon hazy. It diffused its glow. The essence of that glow was carried by Maria's heart as well. She wanted to shine some light on her case, so she sat on her couch and opened her laptop.

She immediately went to check all her social media accounts to refer back to her past. She saw all the tagged photos of her trip that included Alissa and Simone, virtually revisiting her memories. Still, Alissa's profile couldn't be seen by Maria. Yet she could see Simone's profile while her photos were still tagged. Maria thought of connecting with her again. But instead of doing that, she went back to her previous channels of communication with all the three girls. After reading their chats, she then opened her emails. All the conversations between them had been sent to her personal account by the trip company, which was already filled up with a lot of emails. Not scrolling back, she searched for Alissa's name on Gmail's search engine. When all the emails of their chats popped up, Maria went through every single one of them.

It was getting late. Maria had started to feel drowsiness because of her hectic travel and a demoralized trip to Turkey.

Still, the memories of what she had done the past week erupted in her mind in broken spurts. They had become the images of the past, and they occurred whenever Maria lost awareness while reading the emails. Yet her slumberous eyes soon became alert the second she discovered an additional address. It was given in one of the conversations between the three girls. It read: "Name: Alissa Pfenning" followed by an email: "Ip101096@gmail.com". Below that email, there was an address of the location given: "Wiclefstraße 17, 10551 Berlin, Deutschland".

Finally, Maria breathed a sigh of relief and felt a bit relieved that what her boyfriend had explained to her about digging was somewhat true. Yet the adrenaline pump she got upon finding Alissa's email address, that spike of energy, had faded easily. Her eyes automatically began to shut down. When Maria looked at the clock, it was past twelve. She couldn't believe that a few hours had slipped away ever since she had arrived at her home. Her purpose of finding Alissa had become so important that her sense of being felt blind. That being was pulled into the unknown where all the answers weren't given yet. The one clue that Maria thought was in

Alissa's email. The numbers in it made her think that it was Alissa's birthday. Again, broken bits of her thoughts flew past her. Slowly, Maria's attention to her laptop was going away as if her power of volition to dig more was knocked out by this single blow of sleep. After that, she was unable to move because her body needed rest.

The next morning, Maria woke up on a couch. She was intrigued to see her boyfriend resting his elbows on the dining table along with her laptop. "What are you doing?" she exclaimed.

"I saw the address you had found. I ended up searching for the place," he replied.

"Why?" asked Maria.

"Because I want to help you. I know that you are really into it and I know you won't find peace until you get to know what exactly has happened to Alissa. I was thinking about all of these questions until I decided—"

"To do some inspection by yourself?" she interrupted.

Mikael nodded his head. "In fact," he said, "I not only found the location but also called various places in Wiclefstraße 17. I first contacted the bakery there, then a café, and then two restaurants. Do you know what these joints have in common?"

"What?" asked Maria.

"None of them knew who Alissa Pfenning was."

Maria was again disappointed. She saw Mikael's efforts and tried to sway herself from her self-imposed discouragement again towards more digging. After that, she ended up sitting beside Mikael. Again checking the address, she found another piece of information that told her there was a building named Wiclefstraße. The only problem was that it was torn down and rebuilt into an office building. So again, there wasn't any deliverance to her quest. That was what Maria felt when she saw that place in Berlin through Google maps. The rest of the morning and the afternoon were spent reading the rest of the emails that Maria hadn't read upon finding Alissa's address. Whereas Mikael searched more about Wiclefstraße 17 so that he could know the essence of that locality. He thought that the street was decent and would be great for a girl like Alissa to live. When Maria used to tell Mikael stories about what had happened to her in Side, she couldn't let go of Alissa's name. What he determined about her characteristics through his girlfriend was that Alissa was a carefree and funny person whenever she wasn't around Adem. Yet whenever he ended up by her side, Alissa became reserved because Adem wanted her that way. That kind of influence was a sign of wrong domination. It wasn't a loving support that could heal somebody in a relationship. It was a sign of entitlement that might—and could—have led to anger and, perhaps, more.

As Mikael was trying to unravel what might be the outcome of Alissa's disappearance, he saw that Maria had gone to take a shower. When she came back, he went to make breakfast. Thankfully, it was Sunday. If it wasn't, Maria could have been late to the office. By this time, she had read all the emails and she knew every building in Wiclefstraße 17. Yet she still wasn't satisfied. Going back to her social media account, Maria sent a message to Simone to continue to find more information about Alissa. This time, Simone wasn't quick to reply. Maria felt she was running out of patience. She wasn't aware when Mikael put the breakfast plate in front of her like the immodesty of an intruder. While eating it, she continuously kept on checking her phone.

It was after half an hour that Simone replied. She was amazed to hear that Maria had gone back to Side. "Did you find any clues?" she texted.

"I tried my best, but I couldn't find anything about Alissa. Even that damn optician's shop was closed," she responded.

"Now what are you going to do?"

"I have to find Alissa somehow. At least, I want to know where she is and if she is okay or not. Can you tell me more about how long you two kept in touch with each other?"

"For two and a half years; we used to talk. It wasn't often, but we discussed things like how life is going and whatnot. But since then, we haven't talked in years. Whenever I thought about Alissa, I always messaged her, but even her number is now unavailable. Besides, you know that she is not active on her social media. It's strange," replied Simone.

"When was the last time you guys talked?" asked Maria.

"I met Alissa in mid-2017. After we spent time in Side, I never heard from her except for a few days after I arrived back home. I tried to get back to her, but I didn't get any reply. Though when I met Alissa, she looked happy. She was still with Adem, but Alissa avoided answering questions about her boyfriend. Whenever I talked about Adem, his name was the cue for her to end the conversation."

Maria knew that something was wrong when she read Simone's last sentence. She thanked her—whenever Maria texted her, Simone was always there for her, and this time was no exception. Maria knew that if Adem wasn't with Alissa, things would have surely been different by now. Besides, Maria could sense a lot of things about what Simone had to say about Alissa. Maria wasn't feeling secure as she now imagined Alissa with Adem and their trajectory in her mind. That feeling was not there when she saw Alissa for the first time. Looking at her face, Maria had detected a prominent emotion, which was blind love. She now thought that Alissa might have been facing the repercussions of it. Yet some part of Maria's mind was still confused when she again thought about why Alissa avoided answering questions about her boyfriend. Simone was her very good friend, and it seemed like the girls never shied away from any topic. This situation just felt more and more strange to Maria. She again looked at Alissa's email address and then spoke to Mikael, "I'm booking tickets to Berlin."

"Didn't you learn anything this last weekend?" he exclaimed.

"Mikael, I think there is more to the story. Perhaps something bad has happened to her. I don't know. I just get this bad feeling. It just makes me uneasy. Don't worry, this time I will do some more digging instead of losing my strength and giving up."

Her boyfriend sighed and asked, "What about your office?"

"I had never taken enough leaves. I might just do that this time."

Mikael didn't argue much. He knew that she most likely had already booked the tickets, which made arguing about it unnecessary.

Chapter 5

Her instincts were robust. Maria couldn't do anything about it. She met Ahmet, who was very kind to her. Yet when it came to the person sitting beside him, the same courtesy couldn't be seen. It was clear that Deniz wasn't authentic yet wanted to attain that persona to impress Maria. Besides, Ahmet seemed like a tall guy, as he was quite slender like Adem, Alissa's boyfriend. His eyes were dark, so was his hair. His suit was cheap, but under the lights of the club, the suit suited the décor. Among the group, the awkwardness had spread. Adem was protective and didn't speak that much. Ahmet kept on speaking, but his language felt intricate even though he was speaking English. Deniz seemed like that fake person who would ride your tail the entire time if you agreed with him, but if you disagreed with him, tantrums would erupt and he wouldn't be your friend anymore. The only shy girl in the group was the one sitting beside Ahmet.

Her hair was the color of a foxtail. Her eyes were brown and her face spoke of stories, as if whatever she had faced, she didn't want to identify the emotions behind it. If she did, it would break the only steadfast rule of her life.

"This is Aisha," said Ahmet. He introduced her to Maria. Simone and Alissa seemed to know her. They only nodded in her general direction. Maria had extended her hand. "Nice to meet you," she said.

Aisha's eyes squinted towards Ahmet as if in fear. After that, she shook her hand and replied, "Likewise."

"Don't you think it's quite empty here?" said Deniz.

He was loosening his tie while the floating gesture of his hands described why he didn't like the club. There was deliberate negation in his grace, yet that grace had passive sullenness. Looking at his face, Maria thought that it struck Deniz suddenly that nobody saw him that great at all. It was true that Maria did glance at him without astonishment. The club was becoming increasingly empty as time passed. Everybody then decided to go to another club. From one club to another,

Ahmet tried to get close to Maria. Even though she was friendly, her instincts intruded and told her to be careful.

The next club wasn't far away, and it was empty too. But the trio—Maria, Alissa, and Simone—decided to enjoy the emptiness. The club had the usual loud music. The dance floor felt like a slab of concrete. Maria had let go of herself like a carefree child. She had started to sweat profusely too. Simone had that same gesture, so did Alissa. The three girls were finally having fun, and Maria finally felt that her birthday deserved this kind of celebration. It didn't have any fancy festoonery or an expensive dinner. It needed good friends and nothing else. It was later that the trio realized that they were the only ones present on the dance floor.

The three men in their group, Ahmet, Deniz, and Adem, were sitting in the corner of the club. With them was Aisha. Maria had caught a glimpse of her sitting all by herself.

"Hey, Aisha!" Maria called to her.

She looked in her direction. She looked a bit afraid and a bit shy when she met the trio's eyes. They were calling for her to join. At that moment, Aisha's doubtful eyes were directed towards Ahmet, as if she needed his approval. The unspeakable acknowledgement between them at that moment was like his command. Ahmet nodded without any other sign of interest or emotion. Aisha got up, and Maria noticed she appeared relieved. She joined the ladies, but was still a little shy, her eyes full of nothing but the infusion of shyness and fear. Yet, Aisha brought some moves. She grooved slowly and patiently to get on the same track as the trio she had gotten acquainted with. Aisha thought they were best friends who had known each other for a long time. Not long after, the club's initial emptiness began to change as more people started to fill not only the dance floor but also the counter where the drinks were being served.

Aisha began to finally lose herself. When her shyness was gone, she showed some moves as if there was no tomorrow. The sweat that had been released alleviated her anxious persona that had clutched her. She seemed like a different person. It was unbelievable to witness. While dancing, she threw him flying kisses. His eyes had the expression of a blank stare, but it was him having a close eye on her. Soon, the girls dispersed. It was Maria who felt tired and ended up sitting at the counter where drinks were being served. She was taking almost deep breaths while her hair was quite disoriented. In the midst of this, some people stared at her, yet Maria felt nothing but a bit tired.

Because her face was turned in the other direction, she wasn't aware that Deniz was sitting beside her. The second she became aware of his presence; he offered her a drink. His face had the stamp of senility, and his vacant eyes spoke of many things. If Maria had to decide what those things were, it wouldn't be pretty because even though his words tried their best to make her feel comfortable, deep inside she knew that she had to be pragmatic. Instead of gulping a shot, she pretended to take a sip from her water while actually spitting it into that glass. Besides, he was introducing several of his friends. All were men, and all bought drinks for Maria. There was a sharp delineation when it came to buying a drink and offering a drink. It only made Maria's instincts that lingered on suspicion stronger. The introduction of men wasn't one after another quickly, yet it too had its rhythm, and whenever they wouldn't look at her, Maria would take that opportunity to pour the drinks out. She felt quite irritated that, instead of getting to know her, these men wanted to get her drunk first.

For her, trust was vacant at that moment. Suspicion wasn't flung away at all. It triggered her instinct to search further. Her feelings felt stunned by a shock, but Maria's face was all jolly. When Deniz left to talk to some of his friends in the club, Maria was met by Adem. He was careful while his eyes were sizing up one person in sight every now and then. It was Alissa, yet he had arrived from the distant corner of the club to converse with Maria.

"Don't drink what they give you," he said, with his accent. "Deniz and Ahmet are not good guys."

"What makes you say that?" she asked.

"Look at them. You can tell from the way they talk and behave that they're not good people. I was with them just now while you girls were dancing. There is this thing called "man-code". They both don't possess that. They don't know how to talk or behave. Be careful."

"I am," replied Maria.

"But you don't seem to be."

"What makes you say that?" asked Maria.

"You are too friendly," said Adem. "You were talking to these men as if you knew them very well. I will not let anything happen to you girls. But you need to be more careful."

He gave her his care and protection in the form of words, but Maria knew the one person he cared about the most—or tried to control—was Alissa. Other than that, he was cut off from the rest of the world. His only message, in the end, was to not be too kind to strangers. Yet he didn't know that Maria was carrying this façade, and deep inside, she was careful. That's why she didn't have anything to drink because the atmosphere of the club was diffused by the several men she had just met— all of them hitting on her while she pretended to be in their grasp.

Maria noticed that she was no longer sweating and she was feeling a little revitalized. All of this was the aftermath of her dancing. It was the only good thing she had done ever since her birthday had begun. As she sat there wondering when they would leave, Maria spotted another man under her gaze. It was none other than Ahmet himself. He, too, wasn't sitting at his place. Instead, he was accommodating to Aisha now. It was clear she wasn't comfortable with his presence. In fact, far from comforting because he didn't want her to dance anymore, to be herself. But weirdness had a way of spreading in the air. While controlling her girlfriend—that's what Maria seemed to think—his eyes kept on glancing her way. Maria didn't like it at all. Him staring at her every now and then while he smiled felt blatant. His eyes felt like he was studying not Maria's long-lined dress but her figure. His placid frankness didn't have any meaning, especially how he was treating Aisha at the same time.

Besides, Ahmet didn't stop smiling at Maria. Even though, prior to this moment, if she had to conclude his smile, it would be a smile that she might have thought was good-natured. But now, it was without kindness and a bit desperate. Staring at her while being rough with Aisha was definitely not the gentleman's way. Also, it didn't look like the night would be coming to an end anytime soon. Suddenly, the several men that Maria had gotten acquainted with began to file out of the club. Again, the denseness of the club was vanishing. But it was Deniz who followed behind them and told the group to vacate their current club. Everyone listened.

The night was a bit chilly, but they felt warm once they were inside the car. "There is another club. It's the nicest one around here," said Deniz.

He wasn't wrong. The club was impregnable, like a fortress. And near it were parked posh cars, and structures depicted the same aura. The club was packed inside. The people were dancing, and the hall was huge. Maria felt great when she was around Simone, Alissa, and even Aisha. She could see her face wasn't energetic anymore. In the previous club, even though Maria had taken a break, Simone and Alissa kept on dancing. Their modus operandi was to have fun. Maria had the same in her mind, but she couldn't dance the way she danced before. Even though she tried while the men accompanying them, Ahmet, Deniz, and Adem, were lost in the crowd, Maria took breaks intermittently. And when she did, she was again enveloped by the presence of Deniz.

By then, she knew about his fake personality. His shrewd eyes were without any shred of intelligence but a purpose that felt empty like himself. That was what Maria's instincts told her when they again kicked in. Her voice had an intense tone even though she tried to pretend that she was having a nice evening when, again, Deniz began introducing several men to her. Maria was just bumfuzzled and deep inside, stunned as to why Deniz was behaving in this manner. Yet the real reason for the shock was Aisha, who also joined Deniz to introduce the men to Maria. This time, it wasn't the men who were buying Maria drinks; it was Deniz and Aisha.

Maria kept her façade and wondered how Deniz appeared friendly. Under the protection of his smile, he felt like he was delivering results using his fake sarcasm. It was like a confession of his own intent, a secret plea that he didn't want to reveal to Marie. She knew that something was off because she felt that the atmosphere around her was still evasive. Surrounding her were cowardly people who possessed some twisted form of despair. That's what her instincts told her. Its signs could be seen on Adem. He kept warning her through his gestures that were subtle. Also, Maria couldn't sit all night. She eventually joined Alissa and Simone to dance and avoid the men who had been introduced to her.

The trio again danced to the loud music. That experience was untouched by anything else. With them, the night was fun. Without them, it was weird. When the girls went to the bathroom, they were shocked to discover Aisha standing in front of the sink, looking at the mirror and crying. Her mascara had dropped on her cheeks. Her brown eyes were all watery while her face felt hopeless. It was strange to find her in this mode. A moment ago, she was with Deniz, convincing Maria to have some drinks. But now it was Maria who moved forward and put her hand over her shoulder, which made Aisha begin to cry more.

"What happened?" asked Maria.

Alissa and Simone also stood around her to provide some comfort for her sudden breakdown. It seemed as though the growing intrusion of some sort of accident of nature had been hammered into her. Meanwhile, the bathroom had the presence of other women. Some of them recognized her when Aisha spoke in broken English, "I nothing… it's… don't."

It became obvious to the trio that Aisha visited this club often, as eyes turned her way when they passed by. That doubt felt like a certainty when one of the women began to yell at her in Turkish while the other ladies confronted her. It was then Maria spoke, "Hey! What's the matter?"

One of the ladies spoke English. "It's not the first time she's done that."

Maria, Alissa, and Simone were puzzled when they heard this statement. The lady went on to talk in Turkish, again starting to yell at her. It was then that Aisha opened up to the trio. She was afraid of her boyfriend, Ahmet. It felt to Maria that her instinct was finally connecting to a scenario where she would be proved right. Aisha told them she wasn't supposed to speak about her boyfriend at all, but Maria, Alissa, and Simone seemed trustworthy to her, which is why she explained to them her situation. She also added how she had come from a faraway town and how, late at night, she couldn't travel back there. It was Maria who offered to help her.

"You can stay with me for the night," she said.

Aisha then enveloped Maria in her arms. It was then the girls decided to leave right away. When Aisha went to meet her boyfriend, her sad face was like a deliberate offense against him. Yet he kept his cool, and so did Deniz. He had quite a few drinks by this time. Its effect seemed to have been on his voice. It was only Adem who remained the same ever since Maria became acquainted with him. He didn't have any drinks or much to say. All he cared about was Alissa. All he wanted to have his influence on was Alissa. Other than that, nothing mattered to him except if something bad happened to the girls, which it didn't. After using the bathroom and meeting all three of these men, the girls left the club.

There were two cars. Before the gang of them could be divided, it was Deniz who wanted to talk to Maria. He tried to convince her that it was her birthday and that she shouldn't end it the way it was ending, so he asked her to go with Aisha and Ahmet. Maria had made up her mind. She was assertive and she knew how Deniz operated by now. His vibe was disingenuous. Even Ahmet then tried to convince her, in a very subtle way, to come with him so that there would be a division of space between the members that wanted to travel back. All Maria wanted was to be with Alissa and Simone. They had been her original partner ever since she had decided to visit Side.

As the cars were virtually side by side, Maria could see that Ahmet was alone. Besides, Aisha in their car was behaving strangely. Maria couldn't get her intent. She then asked herself why Ahmet would try to control her. She knew he wasn't a good man from how Aisha spoke about him. It wasn't through her words but the feebleness behind her voice that spoke of her fear. Why were they then together? Maria again gave herself another thought. Controlling and instilling some kind of fear felt like the theme of tonight, especially when it came to Aisha and Ahmet, and Adem and Alissa. But with the later couple, one pretended to be a watchful guardian while Alissa danced, and without Adem, she finally seemed to enjoy herself. Yet he was in the vicinity. The same went with Deniz, who was driving the car almost drunk. He seemed to have his way with everything, but was that true when it came to having genuine friends? It wasn't. Simone knew him, and that's why everyone was stuck together in this group. For now, only Ahmet seemed to go away, but it was the girls, all four of them, who decided that for the rest of the night, they would stick together and look out for each other.

Chapter 6

Things were different in Berlin now. It was no longer a city that reflected the remnants of post-war grittiness. However, there hadn't been any variance ever since West and East Germany had dissolved. It was advancing. Historic properties had become the spots for tourist attractions. There were makeovers of many places, whether they were avenues and boulevards such as Kurfurstendam and Unter Den Linden or public squares such as Alexanderplatz, Potsdamer Platz, and Gendarmenmarkt. Maria found a hotel near Wiclefstraße Street, but it was still a bit away from the actual street. It wasn't too posh like in the main city. As the visitors there were not allowed access, it made the hotel quite wallet-friendly. Maria was glad about it.

A little further away from the neighbourhood, was the southwest of the city center. Preceding it was Wiclefstraße. That was Maria's aim. The second she reached her hotel after landing at Berlin airport, Maria was tired. Outside, the evening had a different kind of twilight shade. But her mind was still in combat with the constant reckoning of her past because her aim was to find Alissa. She didn't want to rest. Instead, she just wanted to visit Wiclefstraße.

For some reason, Maria didn't find it surprising that the hotel was commodious. Moreover, most people were nice. The illuminating lights outside had calmed the environment and had made the neighbourhood of Guntzelstraße quiet. That was the vibe. A Jewish population once resided there. After World War II, that population vanished. Yet Maria didn't want to linger on the dark side of history even though these subliminal thoughts intruded on her mind. She had studied about Germany at university whose capital city, Berlin, had suffered from the most impact. Yet now, there was a constant state of change.

The city had an urbanscape vibe. Walking down the street made Maria feel like she was walking on the makeover of post-war architecture buildings that now had a slapdash of multi-cultural aura with the inclusion of bars, cafes, restaurants, and museums. The most common things in Berlin were museums. Even Maria found one while just walking. Yet her aim remained Wiclefstraße. The second she entered there; Maria spotted a restaurant that had a glass-to-ceiling window. The restaurant's name was displayed in neon light above its main door. Without thinking twice, Maria made her way there.

Maria wore a waistcoat. The cold had already made its waves as winter was approaching. She saw her reflection in the window glasses of the restaurant as she headed toward its entrance. Directly approaching the receptionist on the counter, her first question was, "Did anybody by the name of Mikael call you in the past week?"

The receptionist couldn't recall it. Maria gave him a pass. There was also a thought of reservation, but she had let that pass too. After trying to engage with the receptionist and learning about the restaurant, she was sure that Mikael hadn't given a call here. Yet she was still ready to give the benefit of the doubt because Wiclefstraße not only had bars, cafes, and restaurants but also makeshift of more shops and bike paths. What she had seen on her laptop at home felt different in reality. However, the pictures of the streets she saw were taken during the daytime; it was now dusk. It was like the yellow lights had suddenly created new settlements where she had to inspect.

On her radar was a bakery that Maria was sure Mikael had called. The style of the bakery shop complimented the gelato shop beside it. The buildings in the vicinity had red-tile roofs, and now, under Maria's footsteps, the street had changed into handsome brickwork, while previously it was cemented. There was only one person inside the bakery, a lady. She was old, but she was dressed in modern clothes. The decorum of the shop was sharp and colorful. "What can I do for you?" asked the lady.

"Hello, my name is Maria," she replied.

"Lovely to meet you, Maria. How can I help you?"

"Would you tell me if anybody by the name Mikael called here this past weekend?"

The lady began thinking while she tapped her fingers as her elbows rested on the glass shield. After some seconds, she couldn't recall Mikael. It was then that Maria vacated the shop. She then entered a café and inquired about Mikael, but nobody recognized her boyfriend. It made her clueless. "Did he really call them?" she asked herself.

Maria couldn't doubt Mikael because she had noticed his expressions and she knew that he was sincere in his call to help her diligently. If he didn't want to, he wouldn't have sent her yet to another country. Maria then felt the need to sit inside of the café she had just visited, but she continued to walk even though she was feeling tired. Far ahead of her, she spotted tidy front gardens where the bike paths from the street made their way there. If the streets felt calm to her and her body tired, the gardens were deafeningly quiet; not even the buzzing sound of an insect could be heard. It wasn't much of a sightseeing, but that changed when Maria spotted a 20th-century fountain that was gushing with mild water.

She kept on walking in the garden, unable to take her mind off Alissa, who was her primary goal. Besides, a part of her began to wonder whether Mikael had called any bakeries or restaurants in Wiclefstraße or not. Maria kept on overthinking despite the fact that her logical part was telling her that he had, and that the people in the shops probably didn't recognize his name. Maria was feeling exhausted. She walked out of the garden and back onto the street.

She wanted to go back to her hotel because she was feeling defeated and exhausted. Yet she again stopped at another bar and thought to herself that she hadn't inspected that place. The reality was that even if she got to know that Mikael called, it wouldn't have changed anything. It might have changed her perception that he did call, but the current matter was she was bound by tiredness and all Maria needed was a drink.

Clubs were usually dark. The one that Maria entered had that aspect, but the lights there were constantly flashing. She went to take a seat by the counter, the vibe of the new city making her feel foreign. She had also read in the news that Chancellor had allowed a lot of refugees to enter Germany. More than fifty thousand of them had settled in Berlin. She could see that influence in the bar. It was a burst of new energy and a new spark of multicultural dimension.

"Do you need anything?" a voice interrupted her train of thought. Looking up, Maria saw that it was the bartender.

"A martini please," replied Maria. "Add a little bit of mint as well."

The bar wasn't that crowded. Also, Maria felt an element of tension. She saw one guy shouting at another. Due to the loud music, the shouts had subsided. The fight didn't break. The rhythm of this particular bar continued. Inspecting such things from her quick glance, Maria also witnessed a man whose glance met hers. His eyes were observing her even if she was sitting as if Maria had nothing to do but finish her drink. That scene felt uncharacteristically familiar. What Maria observed in the limited crowd of people, she didn't want to participate in. Instead, she felt a bit scared. Almost at the brink of finishing her drink, she was astonished to discover another voice.

"Hey, how do you do?" a man asked.

She turned around, to look at the slightly drunk man, trying to make conversation with her. Maria did not enjoy his vibe. Before answering, she turned to see if the man she glanced at, was still there, but he vanished.

His voice had a husky drawl and he had a big beard. Maria wasn't impressed. A part of her was creeped out because she didn't want to talk to anybody. But the man kept on talking to her. "You seem new here," he said. "I hope the people in the club didn't freak you out."

Maria nodded her head and pretended to ignore him. Her focus seemed to be on the drink, yet the focus was scattered in the semi-wilderness of the club. Besides, the bearded man kept on talking. Her replies were often 'hmm' or 'yes', which also included 'no'.

It felt like eternity. Should she just tell him to leave? He tripped a few times and got awfully close to her.

"Hey sweetheart!" another voice interrupted the drunken man.

Maria and her suitor looked towards him. It was the man Maria glanced at before.

"Yes…?" Maria answered.

"I am so sorry that you had to wait! Work kept me." Said the stranger.

The drunken man stumbled away. Maria was relieved.

"I hope I didn't interrupt, but the guy also gave me a creepy vibe."

"Thanks. Yes I felt that too. Some days I can handle it, but others, I don't know. I guess I just don't have the strength." She answered.

"You're not from here, are you? I can tell by your accent. Are you new in town? If you need someone to show you around, or if you need anything else, let me know." said the man.

"Okay," replied Maria. "Well," she didn't know what to say or how to react first, but she asked, "What is your name?"

"Mark," he answered.

"And how long have you been living in Berlin?"

"Almost all my life," he replied.

"Ah… see… I'm looking for my friend. The thing is, she is lost. I'm trying to retrieve some information about her so that I can find her and perhaps know where she… "Mark got up and left Maria, "lives."

It was strange to see how he left, as if he had suddenly decided that he wouldn't be coming anymore. After a few minutes, Mark was back from another room that was joined to the club. He wasn't alone this time. With him was another man who appeared to be lanky, with a shaggy beard and long arms. He was wearing spectacles, and his shirt was decent. He didn't seem like someone who was into drinking. He was holding an energy drink and introduced himself to Maria as Phillip.

He extended his hand. Maria shook it and glanced at Mark. "I thought you bailed on me," she said.

"No," Mark replied casually. "The second you spoke about data; I knew Phillip could help you. He's very good with computers, and he can help you retrieve some potentially lost data."

Maria was intrigued to hear that. The three of them continued to talk. She could tell that Phillip was awkward during the conversation as he seemed naturally shy. He was a bit funny as well, whereas Mark knew how to keep the conversation going. He was genuine when it came to helping Maria. As the evening progressed, she ended up buying them some drinks and even dinner.

"Don't worry," said Mark. "We will find Alissa. If she is in Berlin, we must dig our way to her. Phillip here," he patted Phillip's shoulder, "will do everything he can."

After dinner, Maria returned to the hotel. She felt relaxed, but a subterranean part of her was also feeling some anticipation. When the next day arrived, her aim was to reach the University of Berlin. That was where Mark had asked her to meet with Phillip—it was a crowded place. On her way to the campus, Maria saw some swaths of lakes and some unbroken meadows. In some streets, she also witnessed some half-timbered mansions that had red-tile roofs. Most roofs had that commonality. On the campus, there were tidy front gardens as well. The atmosphere there was relaxed; the structures were laid out and were not tall.

When Maria met Mark and Phillip, she could clearly see their faces in the sunlight. Even if she had some suspicions, they were quickly dispelled when the men started doing their part to find Alissa. "We need to find a public place," he said.

"Aren't we into one?" asked Maria.

"We need a public place where there is free wifi available and more people involved while there are fewer cameras," said Phillip.

"Why?"

"Because, Maria, we are going to do some illegal online stuff," replied Phillip. Mark turned to her face and said, "Hacking."

As the campus was huge, they had found a place near a cafeteria where all three of them had sat on a bench. In the sunshine of the day, their table was covered by an umbrella. It had given them a shadow and, hence, some anonymity. In no time, Phillip had opened his laptop, and in some minutes, he had found something about Alissa. On the screen of his laptop, she could see Alissa's last Instagram posts. Maria immediately recognized the photos because, in her gallery, Alissa was enjoying time with Adem, her boyfriend. The location was Side. Seeing that, Maria even knew the time of them enjoying their company. The posts were made a few months after Maria met Alissa in Side.

Maria was amazed to discover how fast Phillip was with codes. All he needed was a person's name. And not only had he found Alissa's Instagram, which hadn't been logged in for years, it seemed, but Philip had also managed to get her original email ID. But not only did he get her ID, but he had hacked into it, revealing a plethora of emails full of scams and newsletters. Digging through it, Phillip had found that Alissa had sent herself an email in 2017 in the form of a document. It was addressed to her parents. It read:

From: Ip101096@gmail.com

To: MichaelStamph@gmail.com

Date: 17/02/2017

Subject: My Future

Mom and Dad,

I don't know how to be honest with you guys, which is why I'm writing this letter; the reality is I can't look you in the eyes and tell you I'm in love with someone who you wouldn't approve of. But we're in love, and nationality doesn't matter. The only thing that matters is love. I love Adem. He is from Turkey and he lives in Side. I've decided to leave

Germany and to marry Adem. I will find a job in Turkey. We will start a family. I can't imagine my life without him. I hope you understand why I'm doing this. I really wanted to tell you my dreams for my future in person, but some things require more audacity. Right now, I don't seem to have it. I only seem to see my future with him. I also think I won't return to Germany for some time because Adem has visa issues. But at the end of the day, love is all about sacrifice. I hope you understand my situation, especially Mom. You raised me to be a strong girl.

Your daughter,

Alissa.

PS: I will contact you the second I'm settled. Nothing but love.

There were many such emails that Phillip had found. Maria read every single one of them to discover additional new information that included the names of Alissa's parents, Michael and Diane, typical German names. It turned out that she did find that Alissa had a few connections in Side before they became friends. It wasn't the first time Alissa had visited that place. In fact, she had been visiting Side ever since she was an eighteen-year-old girl. Every trip she made to Turkey, she didn't pay that much money. This included the cost of her flights as well. The reason for such discounts was her contract with different hotels that provided her with some utilities that correlated with the number of trips she had. Alissa had many such trips. The more customers she brought with her, the more discounts she enjoyed. That was why Alissa was quite insistent when she was talking to Maria and Simone before their trip to Side. It made Maria now think of Alissa's persona under a different spectrum of light that evoked skepticism. Yet she was again ready to give the benefit of the doubt because, in her mind, she was determined to find Alissa. Her instincts conveyed to her that she was in some kind of jeopardy, and through the letter that she had addressed to her parents, Maria had gotten to know their actual address. It was in Berlin too, which was luckily closer to her hotel; definitely not a five-minute walk, but a five-minute journey by a taxi.

Hope was lost when Maria couldn't find anything on her trip to Side last weekend, but now her new two friends have revitalized her hope. She was grateful for their help, and in no time, she was quick to depart too, because she aimed to visit Alissa's parents now. She knew that the story now had an enveloping depth. There was more to it, and everything had to

be uncovered.

Chapter 7

Alissa's Parents

So many things were happening. Sometimes the mind felt that it was going cuckoo-cuckoo even though the universe was creating a path. That path was to unravel everything about Alissa. What happened to her? Where was she now? Was she safe? These questions began to intrude on Maria's mind. She was caught up in the whirlwind of events. First, Side. Second, Berlin. Now, her new friends that helped her to find more than something about Alissa. Phillip was a hacker. Mark was his friend and was born in Berlin and knew the streets. These two individuals had become Maria's friends, and what they had found about Alissa was profound. Maria's line of thought was roaming around these spheres as she had taken a bus.

As her hotel was near Wiclefstraße 17, she was going towards the opposite side. The weather had also started to change. Clouds began spreading over the sky and hiding the brightness of the day. Maria didn't care about it. A subterranean part of her felt she should go back to her hotel. But doing that would mean she was giving up on her search for Alissa. At that moment, Maria thought she had to do something about her. Just like her bus had two attributes: motion and purpose, her aim to find Alissa was like that.

When the bus stopped near one of Berlin's metro stations, it began to snow. This transition from a sunny day to a gloomy atmosphere made her body shiver a bit. Going inside the station, Maria didn't feel relaxed. There was an urge to be quick. Many people were there, and all the people felt like countless sudden trails to her that she could follow. Yet the ticket she had purchased on the counter was to Potsdam. It was a city that was on the border of Berlin. Maria had previously heard about the city for its grandness when it came to its structures. The landscape was precise there, with kingly structures. The trees were always pruned to match the appearance of the palaces or churches. Even the normal homes had a 19th-century vibe. Potsdam was once the summer home of the King of Prussia. In today's time, it is a tourist attraction. Yet this was where Alissa's parents lived.

Maria sat quietly inside the train, her eyes observing the window outside with growing intent. It had stopped snowing. Instead, the windows had started to become foggy. Her breath had become visible in the same way. Her lips quivered as the cold seeped in. Maria was glad that, even on a sunny day, she had her waistcoat. She thought she shouldn't have worn heavy clothes as she sat on the campus bench, but that thought was immediately vacated. She was feeling glad that she didn't have to pay attention to how to deal with the cold.

The thoughts of Maria were like pages flipping inside of her mind. There was eagerness that she was finally meeting Alissa's parents. It was like the work that she had done previously and once made her feel that it wasn't giving her any rewards, now finally made her feel that there were a few possibilities that were breaking open before her vision. As soon as the train halted, it was in the late afternoon. Outside the station, her lungs were puffing out her visible breath as if her internal body was some kind of an engine, and the direction of that engine was Alissa's parents' house.

Maria had their address. Besides, the snow had slowed down. A thin white blanket on the ground had changed the look of

Potsdam. The monolith structures were covered in snow. The same was with Italian-style gardens and the fountains surrounding them. All the architectural styles that were composed of different buildings had changed under the white sky. The people were still walking now and were fully covered. It made Maria utter, "They must be returning from their work now."

There were high chances that Maria's parents would be at their home. The second Maria came out of the station, she started to walk. Around her, the city didn't feel like a city. After some grand structures had ended, many lanes paved the way for different streets. Maria knew which way she was going. The street that she had entered was near a church. The different houses in the street all looked the same, with red walls and square windowpanes. The shed in every home was covered with snow. People were walking down the street, and cars were parked by the side of the street—life went on as usual.

Maria finally reached Alissa's parents' house. It was almost in the middle of the street. Maria knocked on the pale blue door and waited for a few seconds, which turned into a minute. When she heard footsteps coming in her direction, she felt anxious. She was surprised when a lady opened the door. She was wearing a sweater. Her hair was blonde and was covered with a cap. Her eyes were brown. She had a medium height. The moment Maria spoke, "Are you Alissa's mother?" The woman's face started to have morbid expressions. The essence of it was like tearing a plug to cut off all the emotions.

"Yes," the woman said, pausing for a few seconds before continuing, "I'm her mother. Who are you?"

"I'm Alissa's friend. I wanted to ask you some questions regarding her."

After again taking some time, Diane answered, "Sure. Come in"

When Maria entered Alissa's house, she felt the warmth, as if the lanes outside hadn't been covered with snow. The living room had a few paintings. There was a fireplace near the carpet where the flames were in a twisting motion. It had activated the chimney, and that was the reason for the current warmth. Over the carpet, there was a dining table. That was where Diane sat along with Maria. She was looking at Maria with an odd frankness. She never thought that something related to Alissa would follow them to their new house.

"Do you want something to drink?" Diane asked.

Before Maria could answer her, Diane got up and went to the kitchen. "Actually, I wanted to have some tea before you knocked on the door. I thought it was Alissa's father who had returned home from work. He will be home soon, I believe. But the kettle is already on, so I'll just make three cups. Let's wait till Michael gets here. We will then discuss what you have to tell us about our daughter."

Instead, Diane brought back two cups of tea in advance. She then spoke, "I never heard her mention the name Maria before," she said, looking at Maria's brown eyes and studying her curly hair. "Would you like to wear a cap?"

"No, ma'am. Thank you. But I'd like to know the last time you saw Alissa."

Diane felt reluctant to answer that question, but she could detect Maria's eagerness. "It was at the end of 2015. By the way, how did you two meet?"

"It was in 2016 that I got to know Alissa in Side," replied Maria. "When I met her, I loved her cheerfulness. She made my trip quite relaxing whenever she cracked jokes and the kind of things you do whenever you are in a group."

"It seems like you girls had fun with her."

"Yes, ma'am. I did."

"Just call me Diane," she said. Sipping her tea, Maria could see how Diane was trying to control her trembling hands. The look in her eyes was as if she had been carried back to the past when her days were alright. Now things were different—until Maria arrived. The thought of the future suddenly seemed oblivious to Diane. There were many thoughts running through her mind that Diane didn't want to pay attention to but felt anyway. It was at that moment that the doorbell rang, and Diane got up.

When the door opened, Maria saw how Michael spotted her immediately, as both parents weren't expecting any visitors at this hour of the day. The late afternoon had turned gloomier. Maria could see from the opened door where Michael Stamph was standing that he was observing her. He had his glasses that complimented his red sweater. The hair over his head was chestnut. He was neither too slim nor did he have a plump body. Michael felt like a university professor to Maria. The next moment, they were sitting next to each other at the dining table.

"How did you meet her?" he asked.

"It was in Side. But I want to know the last time you saw your daughter, Alissa."

Now, Diane's reaction was evident. Her eyes began to tear up. Michael, too, was holding back his tears. It made Maria feel a sense of shock, which she kind of knew would come anyway. It was at that point that Michael began to speak. "After we got our daughter's letter explaining to us that she was leaving us for this guy to live forever in Turkey, it made us worried. But when we decided to take action, we couldn't contact our daughter. I tried calling her, but her number wasn't working. I tried emailing her, but no reply seemed to come our way. Before I could contact the police, one day, at the beginning of 2017, we heard a knock at the door. Nobody was there, but somebody had left a large sum of money. This even included a letter. It was the same letter that Alissa had written to us in the email."

"What happened next?" asked Maria.

"We got worried. We didn't contact the police because of the large sum of money that we had received in the bag. Again, reading the letter, I had many questions. I knew that my daughter was in Side, Turkey. We were quick to make our reservations because even though Alissa didn't exactly tell us about the house she would be living in, we thought we might find her somehow. After several trips to Turkey, we still couldn't find her. We became more worried. We began thinking about the worst-case scenario."

"Why would someone send you money along with Alissa's letter?" asked Maria.

"I think it might be the money that she had saved," replied Michael. "But why she would give away that money, I didn't have an answer for that. We even tried to get access to her bank account, but nothing was working. Even the leads we had in Turkey were dead ends. It messed with our heads. We were confused. Our only child was lost…And we couldn't do a damn thing about it. I wondered if she really was in love. Why was she afraid to introduce her lover to us? It's not like we could have rejected him. In the end, every parent accepts what their children's wishes are. But these events eventually led us to end up in the police station, where we inquired what the people in charge could do. It allowed us to have some media coverage. All the articles, the journalists, and some media channels' coverage didn't have any effect. As the cycle of news never ends, ours got old. People who could help did what they could, but our question was where was our daughter? I just wanted to see her. That's all we wanted."

Diane burst into tears, and Michael comforted her. "They are good parents," Maria thought to herself. In her breaking voice, Diane started speaking. "At the time we were trying to find her, a year went by so quickly and harshly that the building we were living in was torn down. There was a land dispute going on. The builder had lost the case, so the people living in different apartments in that building were compensated. We then bought a new home here. There are fewer people here, and it's more peaceful here. But the peace inside of our hearts has just vanished. All we wanted to do was to see Alissa. I wonder… What has happened to her… is she even…" She couldn't utter the next few words, but Maria knew what Diane was going to say.

As she was sitting close to Diane, Maria took her hand in hers and said, "I promise I will do everything in my power to find Alissa. Don't ever give up hope, even if things seem bleak right now. There is a reason why I'm here. Alissa is my friend. I had wondered what had happened to her as well. After thinking about it and really digging into her whereabouts, it led me here. I can feel you both. I'm determined to find my lost friend."

The parents embraced Maria as she left their house. She could see the pain in their eyes, but she could also see a glimmer of hope as they said goodbye to Maria.

So many thoughts raced through Maria's mind as she headed back to her hotel. Even though Alissa's parents were living, they weren't deep inside. The uncertainty about their daughter's whereabouts and whether she was okay or not made Maria feel despair. That cry inside of her was involuntary until she slowly went back to sleep. The next day, she was woken up by consistent knocking. The second Maria opened up the door, she saw that Alissa's father had visited her. She could tell that he, too, hadn't been able to sleep well.

"Are you alright?" she asked.

"I didn't tell you everything about Alissa. I couldn't open up in front of Diane. If I had, she must have fainted, or something terrible would have occurred. That's why I didn't tell you the whole truth."

For a second, Maria couldn't soak in what she was suddenly hearing. She invited Michael into her hotel room. As he sat in a chair near the window, he immediately said, "Last year I got a call from somebody. His voice was strange, and so was his accent. He told me that if I wanted to see Alissa alive, I needed to transfer around twenty thousand euros, which was a lot of money, so I immediately informed the police about it. We transferred the money, but I never heard from the person who was speaking to me. However, the cops did manage to trace the number. The call was made from Antalya. The only thing the cops couldn't find out was the owner of the bank account we made the payment to. I didn't tell my wife anything about this incident. If I had…That wouldn't be a good thing."

He caught sight of Maria's expression as she thought about her hacker friends. "Do you mind giving me that number and the bank account details? Do you still have it?" she asked.

"Yes," replied Michael, who had begun to check his phone. After a few minutes, he finally found the number and the bank account information. He gave it to her, and Maria explained to him that she should give it a shot this time, and that if she found anything, Michael would be the first to know. That was the end of their meeting. Maria's check-out time was due, but new information had surfaced that couldn't be ignored. She had to find her hacker friends. Even though she knew them, she didn't know where they lived.

As Maria got ready to find them, she also called her boyfriend. The second Mikael heard what his girlfriend had said to him, he retorted, "No! That's too dangerous. What is happening to you? Why are you so obsessed with this girl?"

"Her life could be in jeopardy," Maria exclaimed.

"But it has nothing to do with you. What if something bad happens to you? Just come home."

"I don't have time for arguments, Mikael. I have already made up my mind. Besides, you tell me, did you really call those places nearby my hotel?" There was silence for the next few seconds. "The restaurants? The bakery? Bars? Were you lying to me?"

"You don't know what you are doing. You don't—" he hung up the call. Maria knew that Mikael hadn't called those places; he had been lying. Now confronted, all he could think to do was hang up on her. Maria wasn't sad. All she was thinking about was how to find Mark and Philip. She changed quickly and went to the bar where she had first met them. Not able to find Mark and Phillip, she asked the bartender. "Do you have any idea where they live?"

"Those two guys come here once a week, but I know that they live nearby. Their apartment is close to this building," replied the bartender.

He informed Maria about their apartment. It was just a few minutes' walk, which she had quickly taken part in. Maria stopped when she had reached their apartment. The description of it matched what the bartender had described: an apartment on the first floor down the street with dirty windows. Tilting her head up a bit and standing as if face-to-face with the apartment, Maria spoke, "Mark? Phillip? Are you guys there?"

There was no reply, so Maria decided to shout. "Mark!? Are you there!? Phillip!? I need your help!"

Maria noticed one of the three windows of their apartment slowly opening. She spotted Mark's face and smiled. "Come on in," he said.

Maria gave them all the information as soon as she was invited into their apartment. It had taken a while to do something about that information—the phone number from Turkey and the bank account. While Phillip was doing his thing by typing codes, Mark was sitting next him, his gaze fixed on the WiFi. Maria sat facing them, a curious look on her face. It wasn't long until Phillip uttered, "Got it. Now, tell me. What do we do with the address?"

Chapter 8

It was dark, but with the girls, there was a mere sense of hope. That bond was important, thought Maria. The night was way past her birthday, but still, she felt like more surprises awaited her. Not only were Alissa and Simone by her side, but Aisha was also there. His boyfriend was gone. Even though she was drunk, she felt relieved about it. Yet Aisha's drunkenness had caused her words to slur. The way she then snuggled beside Maria was weird, but Maria had let that go. Aisha's hand was almost touching her lap. Other than her and the other men, Deniz was also drunk. Adem was paying little attention to him. It felt like he was the driver. The only thing missing was the wheels in his hand. Somehow, Deniz was quick to reach the Palm Resort.

When all the girls came out, it was Alissa who went and immediately hugged Adem. He told her that Deniz would drop him off at his location. This idea didn't sound right to Maria,

but in the end, her priority was to be together with the girls.
Her instincts were sensing something that made her feel that
her night was yet to end. The Palm Resort was silent until they
entered the resort and saw that the swimming pool was still
active. The same went with the bar nearby. All the girls wanted
to go to their rooms. Maria was holding Aisha because her gait
wasn't straight. Yet all the girls could feel the necessity of sleep
while they headed to the hotel.

The reflection of blue railings and windows against the white
walls of the hotel allowed Maria to lose her desire for the
night. The hotel's essence was a joy, but what Maria concealed
inside of her was the recognition that it hadn't been the case
for her ever since she arrived at Side. She did grant herself that
it was her experience and she was steering such things. A part
of her also felt that the men that she met today shouldn't be
included, but they were there for their needs, not to have real
enjoyment. The other part told Maria that she should be
motivated by having great girls accompany her, that they made
her have lots of enjoyment.

The main lobby of the hotel was all marble, while the décor on
the ceiling was set in plaster of Paris. The black pillars

complemented it. There wasn't any elevator because the rooms were limited and the building was more square than elevating in height. In other words, the girls took the stairs. It was Maria who asked Aisha, "You should come with me."

Aisha slowly nodded her head and replied, "Thank you."

While Alissa and Simone went to their respective rooms, Maria and Aisha were still walking because Maria's room was on the second-to-last floor. She knew it was more spacious too. That's why she was quite gracious to Aisha. But if Maria had to judge Aisha's body language, it was weird, as if she was displaying the open sores that she couldn't endure anymore.

When they finally got to the room, Maria pointed towards the two beds that she had gotten in her room. One was a double bed; the other was a single bed. While pointing to the latter, she told Aisha, "You can sleep there. Make yourself comfortable. If you need anything, I'll be right next to you," said Maria.

Before she could go to the bathroom to ready herself for sleep, she also saw how Aisha appeared a bit clueless. Her glance then observed her dress. It was tight and it looked quite uncomfortable. Maria immediately checked her bag and gave a comfortable T-shirt to Aisha, which she gladly accepted. After that, Maria went to the bathroom. She looked at herself in the mirror and whispered, "What is going on? Thank God, the night has finally ended."

The reality was that the night wasn't ending. When she came out of the bathroom, she saw Aisha not on her bed but on hers. Maria couldn't lie to herself that she felt awkward and inside of her, there was this constant need for the adjustment that she didn't want to make but had obliged ever since this day had started. But right now, instead of going toward Aisha's bed, Maria decided to sleep right next to her because her phone was getting charged there. She didn't want to take it because there weren't extra plugs available in the vicinity of that other bed.

The second she lay on the bed and closed her eyes, Maria's eyes opened again. Aisha hadn't slept. Instead, she again began her snug. "What are you doing?" asked Maria.

It was at that moment that Aisha kissed her. She was getting too comfortable with her cuddles. "Wait!" Maria said, suddenly realizing what kind of situation she was in. "Why are you doing this?"

"I… thought… you want… this," Aisha replied somehow.

Maria got up from her bed. Her eyes were on the telephone given by the hotel. She immediately called and asked the receptionist if there were any guest rooms available at this hour of the day. It turned out that it wasn't. Maria was clear with her intentions that she didn't want to do anything with Aisha. All she wanted was for her new friend to sleep well and return home safely the next day. Aisha was moved to tears as she listened to Maria's words. In her deep breaths, Maria could sense a deep sigh of relief. It seemed as though a lot of psychological baggage had been dropped off her chest.

"Are you alright? All I want for you is to have a safe night here. That's all. That is my real intention," said Maria.

As Aisha felt relieved, she proceeded to share her story. "Ever since I was small, all I knew was to be a prostitute. When the wrong people come, the wrong desires come too. When I started working as a prostitute, I was a young girl, an early teenager. It was Ahmet who found me and became my boyfriend. He is my pimp too. He introduces me to other men. I spent the night with them. Every week, I spend the night with him too. Every week, I travel to the countryside from my village. It's like one night with customers, one night with him, and whoever Ahmet finds suitable for me. He selects men. When I go back home… It's not good either because I work for Ahmet's cousin. Still, the money is bad. The clients are terrible. Most of them… don't know what respect is… and humility. I wish… I could afford to live in this area… in Side… having fun with real people like you. But I can't… that is sad. It was Ahmet… he promised me that we would get married and settle down here. He would leave this business and we would start a new life here, which keeps me going."

Aisha continued with her story as she again sat in the bed and then slowly rested there. The ultimatum was her going to sleep. Maria was still not comfortable with this. There were so many thoughts that were kept inside of her mind that she didn't manage to go to sleep. Instead, she sat on a chair and looked at Aisha. The next two hours went like this. Maria dozed off, but the reminder that there was someone in the room who had revealed their reality made her come back from her snooze. Also, the reality wasn't making any sense. All Maria wanted now was to be alone and get some good rest. She knew that as long as Aisha was in her room, she wouldn't be able to sleep. Maria began thinking of ways to get this situation sorted out. That solution appeared when she heard the sound of footsteps from the corridor. She knew that the hotel had a standard procedure for those people who were not guests of the hotel but somehow, slept there. They were usually men, but Maria had to do something.

She immediately went to where Aisha was still sleeping and started waking her up. "The hotel's security guards are at the door," said Maria.

The second Aisha heard her, she was quick to get up, as if she knew this type of situation wasn't the first time she'd encountered it. When she rushed out of the room immediately, Maria felt relaxed. Her mind had accumulated so much, but finally, there was an end to all this. That's what she thought. Yet the night was gone by this time. The morning had arrived. Maria only had broken bits of sleep. She then decided to take a shower. Getting ready, it was like her body was protesting why she hadn't had a good night's sleep. Somehow, Maria carried on and went to the lobby again to move to one of the inside restaurants to have some breakfast. Her head was still hurting, but the idea of breakfast gave her a promise of some kind of rejuvenation.

As she passed the front desk in the lobby, the receptionist saw her and halted her movements. "Ma'am," he said.

Maria turned her head. "Yes," she replied.

"A man was here asking about you," he said.

"What?" she exclaimed.

"He is still standing in front of the hotel in his car. He even showed a photo of you," he said and paused. Meanwhile, Maria began thinking that the night was already strange and that the morning seemed to be going in that direction. She didn't want that anymore. Maria was waiting for her friends at the breakfast buffet. Yet here she was, with another hindrance. The receptionist could feel what Maria was feeling, and that was doubtful. "Ma'am, I would suggest you stay in the hotel.

The man in the car seemed a bit shady to me. I wouldn't go out there if I were you. If you can, take the back door."

Maria nodded and thanked him. When she entered the restaurant, she saw that instead of Simone, there was only Alissa and Adem. It was strange too to see her boyfriend so early in the morning—as if he was always connected to her. Besides, Alissa looked alright. Her face was bright with confidence. Maria could discover nothing: whether that gesture was real or fake, she couldn't tell. Yet the note of gentleness from Adem seemed strange and new. Besides, when it came to Simone, she wasn't there at the time. It was Saturday. When Maria sat down at the breakfast table, she enjoyed the Turkish dishes. It made her feel full and as if her energy had been revived. But the thought was still there that told her that a man was waiting for her outside the hotel.

After breakfast, Maria told both Alissa and Adem to leave from the backdoor. "I want to see the beach," she said.

They both agreed, and this time, there was no concealment of any refrain mannerisms from Adem. He seemed to be alright with that idea. So, going from the back door, there wasn't much distance between the actual beach and the resort they stayed in. The sand wasn't golden there. It was dark red with a brown reflection. Meanwhile, the sea was bright blue. Maria enjoyed her time on the beach. Sometimes she would go to the shallow water and play with Alissa as if they were children. Adem was sitting on one of the sunbeds. Some of the buttons on his white shirt were open. His eyes were only on Alissa and nothing else. The other things that completed this landscape were the beach, the sea, and the blue sky where the palm trees whose succession enveloped the second the line of sand of the beach ended.

When Maria was done soaking in her current atmosphere, she sat on one of the sunbeds that were nearby Adem. His eyes were still on Alissa, who wasn't done with her enjoyment. It was the perfect moment for him to say what he had been keeping all this time. "I was the only one who knew Turkish last night. I heard what all the men around me were saying. I was feeling guilty, but I think now is the perfect time to say this," he said.

"Say what?" asked Maria.

"To say that I knew from the start what Deniz and Ahmet were planning. The man who is waiting for you outside the hotel wants to collect money."

Maria had an inexplicable expression on her face. Adem continued. "Aisha was a prostitute. Ahmet was her pimp. He and his guys wanted more money from you because they saw you as easy bait. That's why Deniz tried to sell you to a few people because he thought that if he offered you some drinks, then you would become an easy catch for all his men." Maria was offended by that, yet she maintained her composure. "They thought that if you were drunk enough, everything would be sort of easy, but thank God, it wasn't."

Now, it made all the sense in the world to Maria. She thought her instincts were right after all. If she couldn't see the whole picture before, now everything was clear—why guys kept buying her drinks at the two clubs they had been to, why Deniz kept on introducing men to her, why she was supposed to be in Ahmet's car with Aisha, and why Aisha ended up in her room. It was clear that she had been instructed by Ahmet to spend the night with Maria and, in the morning, collect the money from her. At this point, not only was Maria offended by what Adem had disclosed to her, she was also furious and pissed. The night was stranger than she had thought. Indeed, it was completely the opposite, as if she had journeyed to some oblivious country where she had definitely met the wrong kind of people.

Another thought crossed Maria's mind as returned from the beach—that she was safe and that's what mattered the most. Other than that, her only plan was to return to her country. Yet in the lobby, the receptionist at the front desk immediately eyed Maria. At that moment, she knew that the man waiting for her outside the resort hadn't left. Maria didn't worry because, by now, she had accepted that the whole trip was surreal. Also, the receptionist cared for her. He also had his staff with him. When he nodded to them, they all went to the main entrance and then outside. One of the staff members had conveyed to the man waiting for Maria that she had already checked out of the hotel during the day and was probably on her flight now.

The second the car left, Maria felt safer than before. But was it the end?

Chapter 9

Sitting in Mark's and Phillip's apartment, so many thoughts were running through Maria's mind. Alissa's relationship with Adem felt forced to Maria. There were so many theories had started forming in her mind that she wanted to ebb away. A desolate voice told Maria that perhaps it was Alissa who must have planned to loot her poor parents in this fashion because Alissa and her boyfriend might lack money. The origin of this draconian thought was behind the reason when Maria found out previously that she was invited to Side through a particular site so that Alissa could earn some money. The hotels there wanted more people. Alissa was just helping them, but did that help fulfill her selfish intentions? Maria thought.

Her strange, desolate feelings about her current situation also made her question her own suspicions. Even though a part of her felt ungrateful for Alissa, another counterpoint that Maria gave to herself was: what if Adem had been controlling her? Whatever she knew about that man, she knew he was protective of Alissa. By the looks of his face, he didn't care about the world except for Alissa, and that care obviously seemed like possessiveness. It wasn't good because such overwhelming emotions evoked a deeper part of the persona where dominance towards other people was always triumphant. That wasn't a good position to be in for either the person controlling, or the person being controlled. That kind of relationship was like having friends that treated you like enemies. Here, that person was Adem to Maria.

He was just glued to Alissa, and she might have hacked herself because she was in love. When someone is blind in love, even ignorance appears to be a virtue. The rigmarole of thoughts Maria was having, she thought she was going too far with that. But she couldn't stop making such theories. The most prominent one was this simple idea that Adem must have been controlling Alissa. That felt like the moment Philip shared the address that he had got from the bank account that Maria had given him.

"Twenty thousand euros is a lot of money," said Phillip.

"Yes, it is," replied Maria. "He had the chance to use the payphone, yet he didn't. Perhaps, it was too important to get the money and not see anything."

"Perhaps," said Phillip, looking at his laptop. "Besides, the number you have given us is no longer active."

The thought of whether Adem was controlling his girlfriend or whether both of them might be working together for some kind of scheme disturbed Maria. The moment she got all the information, which was the address, she thanked Mark and his hacker friend, Phillip. They told her that if she needed anything, they would be in this apartment. When Maria left, she couldn't believe that some random people could be this generous. Yet this thought didn't give her any assurance about her current steps. The bottom line was that Maria was determined to find Alissa. That goal had become even stronger the second she saw her parents. They had no idea of what happened to their daughter. A girl, whom they spent 18 years raising, just gone, in the blink of an eye. No contact. And her gloomy whereabouts that they knew of led to not finding anything about Alissa. The idea that she might have been kidnapped was enough to make someone overly stressed.

Living life in that uncertainty wasn't good in the case of Michael and Diane, especially considering their age. Any parent wants their children to live happily. That surety for them was wrecked. Maria wanted to do something about it.

The second she reached her hotel, she didn't want to go back to her country. Instead, Maria had again booked her tickets to Antalya. She knew this news would make her boyfriend even more furious than before. Yet Maria's goal was so concrete in her mind that she didn't care what her boyfriend might think. The moment she knew that he hadn't called the places nearby her hotel, Maria was sure Mikael might be doing such things to refrain from her action. Yet those actions had propelled her more, with a lot of cues and a lot of determination. Everything had become conscious when at first Maria felt hopeless about her actions. She did message Mikael that she was now off to Antalya the next day.

On that very day, she had received a lot of messages from him. This even included a lot of calls. But Maria needed her state of mind to be in equilibrium, so she ignored all the calls while she paid extra for the night to stay in her hotel. She wanted to relax so that she could feel the exposure of her own emotions, which had been released tremendously over the last few weeks. Feeling what she felt was like going into introspection. It provided Maria with a sense of ease. She wanted to soak in the present moment for now. She tried not to delve into thoughts that were obvious to intrude inside of her mind relating to Alissa. What really happened to her? Was she well? Was she still with Adem? Did her boyfriend kidnap her? But why would he do that? If he was so protected, assuming that was his love, why would he go on the path to hurt Alissa? Was she hurt? Was bribing her parents a whole goddamn scheme to live life in Turkey comfortably?

Her mind was picking up questions. She treated herself to a nice lunch and then, afterwards, dinner. All the thoughts had arrived again before going back to sleep. The next day, Maria was off to the airport. Her sleep was much better than in previous weeks. It had provided her mind with some clarity.

The moment she was in a taxi and was heading back to Palm Resort, Maria was glad that her visa hadn't expired. Also, this time she wasn't clueless about arriving in Side. Throughout her journey till now, Maria's actions had provided her with some confidence. Even in the taxi, she was casual as it was a beautiful, sunny day. Her face was devoid of any signs of distress either. The elements of what she perceived previously when she was coming here and now that she was here had a rearranged theme. She knew Palm Resort was close when the palm trees began to pass by the car and the outline of the beach began to appear. Maria knew that Side had many locations such as Aya Sofya, Mount Nemrut, Perge, and Kas, but she wasn't aware of all the seven places. Except for the main street where, Deniz's shop was closed, Maria hadn't explored other places.

That idea was in her mind when she reached her resort. She tipped the driver while Maria felt invulnerable to so many things. She could see that the swimming pool outside was still occupied. There was a plethora of people. Things had started to open again and were not closed anymore. Reaching the front desk of the hotel, Maria also took the map of the city. As she moved towards the stairs after checking in, she was also studying all the places nearby her on the map. It included Cappadocia, Ephesus, Pamukkale, Topkapi Palace Museum, Fethiye, Aspendos, and Dolmabahce Palace.

"Interesting," she whispered to herself.

When she reached her room, she had put the map down. After taking a few minutes' rest, she went to the bathroom to freshen up. When she returned, she studied the map again with courteous deference. But the only problem was that navigating such places required wifi, which wasn't working in the hotel at the moment. She changed her plans to look for the address that she had gotten from her hacker friends. She was sharply dressed, and at that minute, she decided to find the address herself. She took a cab to the countryside. The driver also advised her that if they had taken the opposite route, they would have been at Cirali by now, another less touristy destination.

Besides, it was taking a lot of time to reach her location. When she finally did, her mobile wasn't working, yet she did manage to see the area around her. It had many houses that had smooth architecture. There were also remnants of some old isolated houses. The whole vibe of the atmosphere was strange. It was like some people chose to thrive but stopped; some never tried when they got something. Maria was going through the place, and there were many such places. The bad omen was that her mobile network was lost. The evening had arrived. Maria was tired and wanted to go back to her room again.

The second her mobile received any network, Maria was quick to call a taxi. She stood on the side of the road—at a spot where if too many cars decided to show up, it would create a bottleneck. On one hand, there were houses with dishes and antennas and whatnot. The other side of the road had crops, followed by houses made up of muck and barns, while the light to their house was provided by an actual fire that they had lit. Maria could inhale its smoke until her taxi arrived and she was back at her hotel again. Before she could go to her room, she wanted to grab dinner quickly to quench her pang of hunger. Maria hadn't eaten enough the whole day. When she did, she felt relaxed. The moment she reached her room and opened the door, astonishment seeped into her senses because there was already someone present there that she knew.

"Mikael!" she exclaimed. "What are you doing here?" He was sitting in front of her with his eyes fixated on her, jolting her into shock.

"You got me worried," he replied, but Maria was quite confused as to why he was there out of nowhere. Also, a part of her was relieved that he was present with her. But the questions inside of her mind remained: how did he find her here? What was he doing here?

"You should have called me," said Maria.

"I thought you were going crazy trying to find that friend of yours, so I thought maybe I should join," he replied.

The earnestness in his eyes was weird. It made Maria ask, "Then why didn't you call those places in Berlin? Why did you lie to me?"

His answer wasn't direct. "When I realized you were still determined to find her, I saw there was no way you would return home until you found that girl, Alissa. Yes, I indeed lied about calling those places; but it was because I didn't want you to get entangled in things that might prove dangerous. Besides, your behavior seemed unhealthy. But now…I see through your eyes and feel how it's important for you to find Alissa. I came here because I wanted to help you."

Maria believed him, but still, she questioned why Mikael had lied in the first place. She couldn't get rid of that thought as he began to search for the address that Maria had given to him. The wifi had started to work again, but Mikael's mobile network was also robust. It wasn't like Maria's. A smile appeared on her face when, in little to no time, Mikael found the address on the map. Its resemblance was the same kind of locality that Maria had visited today, and when the evening got darker, she had to leave. On the map, the picture of the house was much clearer. The only thing was that the house wasn't a house but a hut. At least, that's how it appeared.

The next day, both Mikael and Maria started their journey early in the morning. When the afternoon came, they had also arrived at the shabby hut that they had seen on the map. As the day was bright, so did the locality—compact with houses with modern touches except for the shabby hut that was isolated and was on an empty plot that had brown bushes like wheat flourishing out of it. Right next to the hut was a tree.

The front of the hut had bricks that weren't cemented. The door had different writings on it that were crossed. The rest of the walls were white. The second Maria knocked on the door, she didn't know how to react when she saw Aisha opening the door. Both had inexplicable expressions upon seeing each other, but Aisha didn't recognize Maria.

Looking at her face, Maria could tell that she had been through a lot. Her hair was disheveled, her face had lost whatever youth she had previously retained, and her eyes were heavy. Was that remorse? Maria couldn't tell, but before Aisha could slam the door in their faces, she caught a glimpse of her shabby, but modern room. It was a mess with things strewn about.

"Have you seen Alissa?" asked Maria.

No answer came.

"Are you safe, Aisha?"

Still, no answer came.

"Just tell us something," Maria exclaimed.

Mikael immediately knew what to do. Maria saw the way he confidently bent down while taking out his wallet. The second he slipped some money through Aisha's door, she was quick to take it. She then whispered, "Just open it and close the door. Don't say anything."

They followed her instructions and indeed, her home was more than a mess. When they sat on what looked like a chair, Aisha was sitting on the floor casually. She told them that she had progressed in her prostitution career and that the house she was living in was given to her by Adem. His name shocked both Maria and Mikael. They couldn't understand that he was still into this, but Aisha went on to say, in broken English, "He improves… my situation… a lot. Now… I choose my clients." She then laid her eyes on Mikael. "I have got… some more time today."

"Let's stick to the story," he replied.

Aisha explained to them that Adem was a big man now and that the name he had gathered in the last few months for himself was a lot. "He owns… the city," she said, alerting Maria and Mikael, who were listening carefully. They too had doubts because Maria knew Adem's nature and how he was all into Alissa. She just couldn't understand that he was now in the prostitution business. Aisha then told them that he even allotted some homes to the prostitutes who couldn't afford to better their living situation. A place to live and work. "Now… I can even… send money to my family. Last time… this wasn't possible."

She elaborated that she was taking her profession very seriously. She had taken many short courses so that she could improve herself in the long run. But looking at her, both Maria and Mikael could tell that nothing, in the long run, would prove fruitful because Aisha was lying. It was obvious that she had succumbed to drugs. Her face even had some white patches.

"Can you tell us where Adem is?" asked Maria. "Do you know where Alissa ended up?"

These were juicy questions that made Aisha quickly show the money that Mikael had given her. It meant she needed more. Mikael took out his wallet and handed her some more notes to utter her story. "I saw her a year ago," replied Aisha. "I don't know… if she is into prostitution… or what she is doing now. She might be with him… because I used to always see her with him." She even conveyed that she hadn't seen Adem in a while either because he was a busy man now. Even if he had to meet Aisha, he would come once a month just to inspect her house. But every week, he would send a man to collect money from her. Aisha was about to say something when they heard a sudden screech of a car's tires outside of her house.

"Go! Now!" Aisha whispered intensely.

Maria and Mikael exited quickly through the back door. The intensity of the afternoon was a lot as they scurried off to some random street. In their minds, all they had were doubts. So many questions popped up until they finally stopped to discuss the situation.

"What do you make of all this?" asked Mikael.

"I just don't understand how Adem became this guy—as if he is some mafia," replied Maria.

"If Alissa is with him, then why did they blackmail her parents?" Mikael asked.

"Perhaps, he needed the money to start this prostitution business or expand it. Just the thought of that makes me sick," Maria said, as she began walking towards Aisha's shabby hut again, when Mikael clasped her wrist. "Don't," he said.

"We need to find Adem and Alissa," said Maria. "But first, we need to inform Alissa's parents of everything that we have discovered. We need to tell them about our findings."

"Don't," Mikael replied again. "First, let's discover what we have got on our plate. Let's not get our hopes too high."

Chapter 10

Whatever Adam had to say about Deniz's knowing what was going on in the clubs had made Maria worried. Deniz was trying to make her a customer, and the idea that he was trying to "sell" Maria to other people was draconian. It was without her acknowledgement while he was trying to make her drunk on purpose. That wasn't acceptable to her at all. On the other hand, there was a car waiting for her. The man inside thought that Maria had most probably slept with Aisha and now he had come to collect money from her. He was thinking Maria had finally spent the night with her. Yet the guy on the front desk had understood the situation well enough and, using one of the staff members, he had vacated that man. It made Maria think about the aftermath of her birthday in her hotel room.

Even though the man in the car was told Maria had left the hotel, she hadn't. After what Adem said to her, Maria decided to go to her room. Even though she had a lovely time on the beach, she still couldn't get rid of her thoughts. It wasn't that there was fear inside of her, but understanding the depth of her situation had given her perspective more to think about. That's what she was trying to do, even if there was still anger inside of her. She had grown to dislike Deniz, even though she knew from the start that he was a phony with nothing to offer. Maria was perplexed by his treatment of her as if she was some foreigner, as if she was an abstract principle who would not understand the environment and of which he was taking advantage.

Deniz's gesture of impertinence was sickening. It was without moral action and moral righteousness. It made Maria, in her room, launch into a speech of explanation. Maria's flight was at 1 o'clock in the morning the next day, but today, after breakfast and spending some time on the beach, she was lying flat on her bed. She wasn't afraid of anything. The experience she had had in the last two days, including today, was like a gun aimed at her. She began thinking about Alissa and Adem. She then thought about why Simone left suddenly. Counting these things in her mind, she dozed off.

Sometime in the afternoon, Maria heard a knock on her door. Waking up and feeling that her sleep had been restored, Maria was quick to open the door. She was surprised again to find Simone. Beside her was Alissa. Maria quickly invited them to her room. Simone's features seemed to lose their delicate sharpness. It made Maria worried. "What happened to you?"

"I just lost track of time," she replied.

"What?" Maria exclaimed.

"Simone hasn't been resting properly during this whole trip," said Alissa.

"Yes, I haven't been resting. Perhaps that's why I became careless while thinking to myself that my flight was today. It wasn't," said Simone.

It was hard for Maria to grasp what her friend had done. She had arrived at an airport early in the morning only to find that her flight wasn't even booked. It was strange nonetheless. Besides, Simone did need some rest from the looks on her face. After getting to know what had happened to her and how she returned to the hotel, another topic of discussion had begun.

"They were trying to get you drunk so that other men could spend the night with you?" exclaimed Simone. "Am I hearing this right?"

"Yes," replied Maria. "Those men were friends of Deniz's. He, along with Aisha, began serving me drinks. Thank God, I didn't drink and discarded them."

Simone didn't hear what Maria had to say about Deniz. "He is never like that," she replied. "But I'm ready to give the benefit of the doubt."

"Do you know what kinds of activities he involves himself in other than the optical business?" asked Maria.

"I never indulged in observing him. But whenever we met, he was always nice to me and he always helped me," responded Simone. "But you are alright," she said to Maria. "That's what matters the most. If those men were really into making you drunk, then thank God for your smartness."

"But the story doesn't end there—"

"You know what," interrupted Alissa, who was looking at both faces of her friends, and she felt the conclusion of their conversation wouldn't be a cordial one. "Let bygones be bygones. After all, we are all together now. Let's have some fun."

All the girls had spent time together in Maria's room. Soon, the afternoon had turned into the evening. The girls had started to feel hungry while their topics had now changed from speculation to random discussions. It was like, subliminally, all the girls had decided to keep peace among each other by changing the topics. The next moment, all were having dinner. This time, Adem accompanied Alissa. Seeing him again and knowing that he stayed with her and was like glue tied to her, the pairs were like one couldn't live without the other. Besides, Alissa never really objected to his presence. On the other hand, Maria didn't feel like she was compromised anymore because now, without Adem, the group would feel incomplete.

As they were having a lovely dinner, Alissa started to become sentimental. Her eyes then became watery because her flight was at 4 a.m., three hours after Maria's. Tomorrow, it would be Simone who would be left alone in the hotel without the other two girls, Maria and Alissa. Anyway, they all had a lovely dinner. Simone and Maria comforted Alissa and told her that they would be meeting again. It was right after dinner, and everyone parted ways, except Alissa and Simone. The couple went to their room. Maria and Simone went outside to have some fun. In the back of Maria's mind, she knew if she was fearless, she still had to be careful.

Just when they were about to start their walk, they spotted a car. It was a blue Trabant built by the Communists in East Germany. They could tell that the car lacked a powerful engine. And by the looks of that car, it looked like it had never been to a repair shop. For a second, Maria thought that these types of cars were available in kids' stores. The only difference was that those cars were way too small and the car before her was somehow bigger in size. It was Simone who took the picture of the car, thinking that nobody was inside it, but the flash revealed a person. He was quick to get out of his car. A thought had arrived inside the duo: Simone and Maria, that they shouldn't have done that, but the owner of the car was jolly.

"Hey, do you want a ride in this car?" he said.

Simone looked at Maria. "You don't mind?" she asked.

"The car is not that much appreciated, but I think you girls seem to have some odd fascination with it. Anyway, tell me if you want to have some fun with it. I wouldn't mind that."

Looking at the guy's friendliness, the girls hopped in. It was Maria who was driving the car. The engine sucked. The car seemed to shiver as it moved forward. The owner was sitting in the back seat. He had introduced himself as Ayaz. "Even though the car didn't have a good reputation, its production continued from the 1960s to the 1980s," he said.

"Well, that's good to know," Maria replied.

After just a few minutes of the girls driving the car straight, Ayaz again spoke, "I forgot to tell you something," he said.

"What?" Maria asked with a bit of worry in her tone.

"I repaired the brakes, but be careful…Don't trust the brakes that much. They are still not properly fixed yet."

Upon hearing this, Maria slowed down the car even more. It was now engulfing a bit of traffic around them, but no one was following the rules. Ayaz was sitting casually and chilling while watching the girls drive. Even Simone was okay with the traffic. It was then that Ayaz said to Maria, "People in this part of the town don't follow many rules when it comes to the traffic light. Welcome to a third world country."

The volume of traffic had began to increase. Even Simone was starting to get a bit nervous. People were driving around with no care in the world. Meanwhile, Maria was thinking that whenever she drove by this place, she was in a taxi, but this was a new experience. Besides, the car she was driving was like a death machine. It could only slow down, yet the cars around her, most of them didn't have any plan of slowing down. Their motive was to get ahead, no matter what. But deep inside, in the midst of all of this, Maria felt adventurous. Ayaz just at the back, relaxed.

"Don't worry," he said. "Welcome to the real world. When I started learning to drive, I was like you. But slowly, I learned my way through a lot of mistakes. I once flew over to a pavement and smashed into this open restaurant, but luckily, people weren't there. The police arrested me, but I got out on bail. Soon, the charges were dropped and I became a free man once again."

"What do you do for a living?" asked Maria, handling the wheel.

"I run many businesses as long as it makes sense. The moment it starts to bore me, I hand it over to someone else," he replied.

"Then why are you still driving this car?" asked Simone. "You could have bought something amazing."

"But if I had done that, I wouldn't have met you girls and we wouldn't be in this mess," he chuckled. "I'm kidding. Besides, the reason why I don't have expensive cars is that even if I have some money, I value my experience. I value everything except the money because I know it will arrive somehow. When I crashed on top of that restaurant, even though I got bail, the police had their eyes on me. I had to drive by hiding my face, which meant hiring a driver. Then I found someone who worked for the police. It turned out his salary wasn't all that pretty. I then started paying him more. He was the one who suggested to me that I shouldn't use just average cars but below average. Before the incident, I never used to have a craze for expensive cars. I was broke at that time too, but after making some money, I decided to buy normal cars. And now this."

Ayaz kept on telling his crazy stories. Maria was driving carefully and much slower. Besides, he felt genuine. Whatever he told them was like he had nothing to hide but only to share. When the traffic slowed down, Maria then saw his face in the rear-view mirror. He had a nice head of hair and he looked to be in his late forties. He wore a coat that looked like a blazer. His shirt and pants were both black. There was a watch on his left wrist. That was the only thing that looked expensive. His eyes were neither dark nor consisted of different colors. It was black but light. Whatever he had to say, everything matched his face. There was neither the defiance he seemed to be displaying, nor any regret. The same goes with any kind of shame or suffering. These things didn't seem to have any impact on his life. His vibe was just chill and carefree. It also sparked neither excitement nor joy; instead, calmness. Also, Ayaz was trying to make everyone calm. It was then he asked, "Do you girls wanna go to a club?"

The duo had agreed to him. That was when the car stopped. The first place that he took them was a solo bar. Ayaz bought them a few drinks that were light. He told them to start slowly and then pick up their drinks in moderation. In his mind, he had many places for the night to visit. That's what Maria and Simone perceived. They were right when, right after the bar, he took them to a club that was on the opposite side. The club was all flashy and the sign outside of it was in Turkish, yet the vibe inside was chill like Ayaz. The girls didn't seem to have any problem when it came to booking a table. The bartenders knew Ayaz. The guards standing at the main entrance knew Ayaz. Even the owners of that bar and that club knew Ayaz. It added some credence to his story that he wasn't lying.

Simone had also let go of herself. She danced, and with her, Maria did too. Yet Ayaz was relaxed in his head. He had his careful eyes on the girls, like he was protecting them. But even the girls knew that after a few hours, they would have their respective flights quite early in the morning, so they had to be collective. Also, when the girls were done dancing, they saw that in Ayaz's seat, there were men. Ayaz introduced them, and they too had the same resemblance when it came to manners. They were calm in some ways and seemed to enjoy Ayaz's company. After their introduction, the men slowly left. Ayaz then took the girls to another club. Again, there was no problem when it came to booking the table. Somehow, Simone and Maria felt protective because Ayaz knew his way around. It was then he spoke to them, "If any man offers you a drink, don't take it. Another tip would be to always buy water bottles that are closed. If you do want to have some drinks, then let the bartenders give them to you, not the other people. It's very important to not loose-guard."

What he said to the girls made them admire and respect him even more. Ayaz then went on to continue how Turkey was a great place for tourists, but some places were really great at scamming people. Side was one of those places.

"How long have you been here?" asked Maria.

"Almost all my adult life. But I do like to visit the city. Istanbul is a great place, but as things are starting to open up again, I might go there. You wanna come?"

Maria knew he was kidding. "I'm leaving tonight," she said. "But one day, if I come here, I might go to Istanbul first."

"Me too," said Simone. "Also, everywhere you went tonight, everyone knew you. How is that possible?" she asked.

"It's simple," replied Ayaz. "I give the people the respect they deserve. They give the same respect back. Treat the men as you would want someone to treat you. I did the same to you girls tonight. I realized you loved the car, so then I asked myself, "Why don't I ask them to drive it?"

The girls began to laugh. Simone, Maria, and Ayaz seemed to enjoy each other's company. They all started wandering into random topics. Time started to fly fast. But suddenly, Simone's expression began to change. Maria wanted to ask what was going on with her. At one point, it seemed like it was only Maria and Ayaz who were genuine when they talked about the tourism situation in Turkey. Simone was just a mere participant in it. Slowly, she was just driving away from the conversation until Maria saw what was happening to her. It was her phone that kept on buzzing and that Simone kept on ignoring. The caller ID had Deniz's name. Maria was taken aback, but the real shock came when Deniz appeared out of nowhere in the same club where they were.

The second he saw Maria, Simone, and Ayaz together, he just turned back and left. It was a very strange situation. Maria's head had begun to spin; not because she was afraid of him, but because the thought of confronting him had entered her mind. It made her feel like perhaps that's why Deniz left the club in that manner. Meanwhile, Ayaz was just calm, and his vibe was just chill.

Chapter 11

A New Shop - with the Same Face

The sun was still sharp. Both Maria and Mikael were tired and needed to eat something. They had ordered a taxi, but they ended up stopping at a nearby restaurant because they wanted to relax and drink some water. The restaurant they had stopped at was okay. After drinking some water, they ended up ordering pizza and a glass of beer because that's what the place had to offer them. Both of them felt as if they were on vacation. The birds were chirping, and the sun warmed their skin. Nonetheless, the matter in which they had become involved was serious.

"What do you think we should do now?" asked Maria, as she took a sip of her beer.

"First of all," said Mikael, "We've gotten mixed up in something deep. Whatever Aisha had to say about Adem was not good. If he's running a prostitution business, he's probably involved in something nasty, like human trafficking. I wonder what Alissa must be doing."

"Aisha said that she had seen Alissa a year ago with Adem. The question would be: is Alissa still with him? Plus, that car had stopped outside Aisha's house. It must be one of Adem's men who might have come to collect weekly payments or to check on her." said Maria.

Both were in deep discussion, but Maria's instinct still couldn't shake Mikael's lie about calling those places in Berlin. And now, Maria was wondering how he knew to give Aisha money so that she could give them information. Many such doubts kept on coming that Maria was trying hard to ignore. But she had the self-control to not raise such concerns at the moment. She would do that later on, she thought, because Mikael proved quite helpful as he was the one who was able to find the shabby hut and, ultimately, Aisha.

As they were eating and talking, Maria tried connecting her mobile to the restaurant's wifi. The second it got connected, she received a notification. Checking it, she saw that her hacker friends from Berlin had messaged her. "Hey, we did some more digging and might have found Deniz's address. It was hard to trace him since he had closed his shop, but he was quick to open another shop right after the first one closed. Deniz B is the owner's name of his new shop. As soon as we found it, we thought of informing you." Below, the message read, "Just click here to see the place on the map. Good luck and keep us updated."

Maria was quick to open up the link. The map directed her to a place in Side. Mikael was reading her expression, and when she showed him the mobile, he was quick enough to book a cab. It was still afternoon, and they weren't tired enough to stop their quest to find Alissa. Besides, they had to fill the day. Reaching Side hadn't taken a lot of their time. The new place where Deniz's store was now had fewer crowds, but the houses were still compact there. Some trees had flourished like flowers and were part of the lanes. On the other hand, Deniz's shop was now smaller than his previous shop, which was now closed.

It was obvious that the years had gotten the better of Deniz, but he still had that familiar smug look on his face and that smirk that had irritated Maria the first time she saw him. That smirk had brought the memories of his antics back into Maria's mind and had angered her for what he tried to do to her that time. But Maria took a breath while she and Mikael were acting like they were on vacation because it was Deniz who had immediately spotted them. He was also quick to say, "Hey, what are you doing here?"

"We are on vacation," she replied. "Anyway, as we are meeting again somehow, I would love to know if you have seen Simone or Alissa lately."

When Maria asked him this question, he invited them into his store. His morale was down. His eyes looked sad. His body language had crumbled a bit. "Simone and I broke up in 2018 because she decided to stay with her husband. We were just having a vacation fling," he said, "but my feelings got compromised. Plus, I wasn't able to take care of my finances. I was too much into these kinds of things instead of paying attention to my business. That's why I ended up shifting my place, but there is more. When I wasn't able to afford the rent of my previous shop, let alone the protection money, Adem came to help me. I desperately needed a job and he was there for me for around two-three months until one day he just disappeared. It was weird. After some time, I started hearing about him. I got to know that he worked a lot and was starting to make a name for himself in Antalya. But I chose to stay here because it was much safer here—in terms of business and people."

"Why?" asked Maria.

"The business is much better in Side," Deniz replied.

Maria was fighting back her anger as she listened to him. Deniz was talking to her and Mikael as if they were his friends. Yet Maria was controlling her anger because she could remember that the last time she had seen his face, Deniz was trying to sell her to other people because she was an "easy" catch. Those flurry of emotions that weren't gone but were just deeply buried again had started to erupt inside Maria. She tried to maintain her calm manners while getting out all the information from Deniz. Yet she couldn't feel reluctant. Things were just stirring up inside her. She then just exclaimed in the midst of him talking, "Why were you trying to sell me to those guys the last time? Why would you do something like that?"

Her sudden outburst caught Deniz off guard; he didn't know how to respond or react. He wasn't sure of what to say. He felt awkward because he knew Maria was right. Not able to talk his way out, he began saying, "You see… I wasn't trying to…" he then began mumbling his words. It was at that point that Mikael interrupted him. "See, we are not here to create a scene or to rat you out. We just want to know how Maria's friends are doing now."

When Deniz began to speak again, he got a bit emotional. "Everyone has to start somewhere. In this place, if you've already made a name for yourself, then you are in a better position because it's really hard here. Every area is somewhat occupied by an influencer. If you want their protection, whether you like it or not, they all love to get paid. From the smallest gangster to the highest boss, it's how things work around here. At every level, you will meet such men. They control their space and they make their own rules. I didn't want to be that because I saw how things worked around here. It was pretty hard and I was stuck. I knew everyone wanted the money, while I had to start from below, at the bottom of the food chain. Besides, I never wanted to have a family here. I knew that if I did, they wouldn't be safe here. That's why I wanted to go to another country. That's why I tried to find a woman that would take me out of this country, but I haven't met that person yet. Somehow, I feel that I would die alone here without having any family. The government had also taken my passport. I couldn't afford the spot for my old shop," his voice began to break, "The rent was okay, but when it came to the protection money, it was too expensive. So, when I began to lose everything, I did all sorts of shady things to survive. I stole from people and scammed tourists. Sometimes I was too hungry," Deniz began to cry, "and stealing from people and all these shady things usually didn't work out. I'm not proud of it. I just feel sad that I did such things. All I wanted was to leave this country, but I never made it out. Perhaps I never will."

Both Maria and Mikael didn't know how to react to this. His tears seemed genuine, and so did his story. However, his expression suddenly changed as he said, "I'm going to a party today. Though I didn't want to go, as things seem to be going well, but there would be all sorts of activities." He offered them to join him. His mood was suddenly enlightened, as if

Deniz had never shed his tears a few moments ago. Instead of talking about activities more, he took out a brochure and offered it to them. On it was a picture of a sunset ride that also had a party on the boat. Maria presumed that this was where Deniz was going. Besides, the smirk on his face was back. Deniz was also back to normal, and it was strange to see that his mood had changed so suddenly.

Maria thought of ignoring what he had to offer. Mikael was feeling the same too. Instead, it was Maria who interrupted and asked, "Do you know where to find Ayaz?"

Deniz was a bit shaken when he heard that name. Suddenly, he remembered seeing her and Simone with Ayaz. That was also the last time he had seen Maria, thought Deniz. "Ayaz was involved in a car accident about a year or two ago. For some reason, that idiot kept on buying old and broken cars. One of them was a total wreck, and he was still driving in it. But eventually, he had to face the consequences because he was found dead in his car, quite far off the road. He sustained a few fatal injuries, but I'm not sure what killed him in the end," he said. Deniz felt a bit enthusiastic about it. There was a satisfied look on his face, which was sickening. "His car collided with a big rock. The news covered it, but then everyone soon forgot about him."

Maria didn't like hearing what had happened to Ayaz. She liked him and thought that if she could have met him again, things would have been slightly different. Yet that perception was changed when Deniz continued speaking, "I don't know all the details, but Adem and Alissa were involved with him. I also heard a rumor that Alissa used to spend a lot of time with Ayaz before his death. Well, who am I to know this reality? I just tried to keep my distance from them so that I could live my life here in peace."

"How were they involved with Ayaz?" asked Maria.

"You don't know?" asked Deniz.

"Know what?" said Maria.

"That Ayaz was a gangster?"

Maria looked at Mikael and they both shook their heads, telling Deniz that she didn't know what Ayaz was up to. Due to this, Deniz was taken by surprise, but anyway, he spoke, "Ayaz was a criminal genius and, somewhat, a mafia boss. He

154

ruled the coastal area from Antalya to Mersin. That's why you must have seen that time in the club when you were with him that people seemed to know him. Also, he had many people working for him. Some feared him; some adored him. Besides, he had a way with strangers when it came to talking to them. He knew how to be interesting and calm. That's why he made it easy for tourists whenever he met them and conversed with them. That quality of his was fascinating. He was either your friend or your worst enemy. But most of the time, Ayaz was reasonable. Almost everyone knew that one shouldn't mess with him. If one did, the result wasn't pretty. That's why when I saw you and Simone that evening, I left because I saw you two girls with him and I was afraid. I didn't want to mess with him."

It now made Maria think back to when Ayaz was telling them he was into so many businesses. All his crazy stories now had a particular reason behind them. Knowing that he never had any interest in buying expensive cars was a way for him to hide well. He was once chased by the police, and then he ended up crashing his car into an open restaurant. All this led to him buying cheap cars and whatnot, which now had its conclusion that Maria didn't like. As far as Ayaz's character was concerned, she knew he was a genuine guy, and so did Simone. And now, Maria also understood why her expressions began to change in the club when Simone was receiving a lot of messages and calls, which she ignored because Deniz was her boyfriend at that time. That's why Simone also couldn't believe it when Maria told her that time in the hotel room what Deniz tried to do to her. It all made sense now. Yet, Maria was still confused because there was nothing significant about Alissa.

Also, Maria and Mikael had spent too much time in Deniz's shop than they had anticipated. Thanking him for his time, they left the place. It was still late afternoon and in the cab back to the hotel, the first glimpse of the evening had arrived. The day had so much to offer, but not so much about Alissa, yet there was more hope than ever before. The hotel was also quiet; it wasn't a rush hour, it seemed. Besides, the couples were tired. The last meal they had wasn't the most nutritious— pizza and beer. So they decided to eat a proper dinner at the hotel's restaurant. Maria and Mikael wanted to start the next morning feeling refreshed, so after dinner, they went to bed and retired for the day.

Chapter 12

Ayaz didn't even care that Deniz had arrived at the bar. Meanwhile, Deniz, seeing Ayaz with Simone and Maria, just turned around and left. He never returned, and Maria felt relieved about it. But she couldn't say the same for Simone. Her expressions were still changed. Maria couldn't detect any excitement on her face, only worried expressions. Maria didn't want to see Deniz's face after what he had tried to do to her. She was still angry, and Ayaz could sense her anger.

"What happened to you?" he asked.

"Nothing," she replied. After taking a pause, she asked, "Why did that guy just turn back after seeing your face?"

"He must have mistaken me," replied Ayaz.

"For what?" asked Maria.

"It doesn't matter. On this side of the place, there are all kinds of people and all sorts of connections. That man must have thought that I might be the wrong guy to mess with. Well, that's perception. If he thinks that, I can't do anything about it. But it seems like you knew him." Ayaz was looking at Maria's eyes intently. "Did he do something to you?"

"Yes," replied Maria, in honesty. "I met him yesterday and he was trying to intoxicate me… and tried persuading me to talk to other men. His intentions weren't right. I didn't know at that time that he had such intentions, but I got to know about him."

"That's not good. Now, stay away from him," said Ayaz, who then turned to look at Simone.

He realized right away that the subject Maria and he were discussing was bothering her. Nonetheless, she remained silent. After a while, she excused herself to go to the bathroom. The music was loud in the club, but the moment Ayaz saw that Simone had gone to the bathroom, he spoke, "Does Simone have anything to do with that guy who had just walked into the club and then turned around?"

Maria nodded her head and said, "I couldn't tell you this properly, but he tried to sell me to other men so that I could spend the night with them. That's why Deniz tried to give me so many drinks, but I didn't drink any of them."

"You were smart," said Ayaz. He then made a strange face. Ayaz almost started to laugh. "You said his name is Deniz?"

Maria shook her head, and she saw how Ayaz was taking him lightly. "Do you know him?" she asked.

"I just don't care about him. I don't care about anyone unless they are related to my businesses," he said.

Before Maria could say anything more about Deniz, she saw Simone coming back from the bathroom. Her face didn't have worry anymore, but it didn't show any sign of happiness either. She put on a straight face, and she was quick to remind Maria that it was getting late. Meanwhile, Maria had changed the subject with Ayaz. He was very cordial. It was then that Maria checked the time and agreed with Simone that they indeed were getting late. Ayaz also got up and was about to offer his help until Simone spoke, "Alissa must be waiting for us."

"She must have slept," answered Maria. "Plus, Adem is with her."

"Who is Alissa?" asked Ayaz. "And Adem?"

"Alissa is our German friend, and Adem is her boyfriend," replied Maria.

"A Turkish boyfriend?" exclaimed Ayaz.

Simone nodded her head. "Yes, they must be waiting."

"I think I have heard his name before," said Ayaz.

"Who? Adem?" asked Maria.

"Yes," replied Ayaz. "Do you have his picture? I might know something about him."

Maria examined Simone's face. She, too, was curious. Maria then took out her phone and showed a picture of all of them together, including Alissa and Adem. Ayaz didn't recognize the picture Maria had taken the other night, but she was quick to tell him that Adem had visa issues. "He is desperately looking for a job," she said.

"Is that so? But how—"

Before Ayaz could complete it, Maria replied, "Alissa comes back every month or two to meet him. They think that their relationship will work somehow. Well, I wish them the best."

It was clear that they were drifting away from the topic of returning to the hotel. When Simone showed Maria the watch, pointing at the time, Ayaz was quick to lead them. He had offered them a ride, but this time he drove. Ayaz had remained a perfect gentleman by looking after the girls and allowing them to enjoy what the evening had to offer. When they got to the hotel, only Maria got out of the car. Simone then told Maria that she was going back to Deniz. Maria then figured out why she had looked worried when her phone started buzzing with calls and messages. It was also clear why Simone didn't really like it when Maria spoke badly of Deniz. Ayaz, however, didn't look surprised. He drove Simone to Deniz while Maria went back to her hotel room all tired.

In two hours, she had to leave. After some time, Maria also received a message from Simone saying that she had returned to the hotel as well. Both the girls were tired in their room, yet their chatting didn't stop. They both decided to sleep for two hours before leaving. They still hadn't informed Alissa about it, thinking that she might be sleeping. Simone and Maria didn't want to disturb her. That's why they didn't say goodbye to their friend. The funny thing was that they overslept, but they decided that they would board the flight somehow. So, in the morning, Simone and Maria met in a restaurant and told each other that Alissa must be upset with them because they couldn't say a proper goodbye to each other. They thought Alissa must be sad too because they had received so many missed calls from her. Both the girls then tried calling Alissa. After that, they texted her, but there was no response. It made Simone and Alissa think that Alissa must be on her flight.

Not worried about her, they went on to catch their flight. Half an hour later, while on the plane, Maria received a text back from Alissa. It read: "It was a lovely experience with you guys. I had a great time. I wonder if we can meet again in Turkey. It was one of the best trips of my life."

Maria texted her back, saying that she enjoyed spending time with her. Even though she was glad for Simone and Alissa, Maria knew deep down that she wasn't glad for every experience she had in Side. When she finally reached her home, Maria was exhausted from her weekend trip that didn't feel like a weekend but more. All she wanted to do was rest. Thinking of her experience again after she rested and when she came back to her normal schedule, Maria was sure that she didn't want to go back to Turkey again anytime soon. That intent was lost. Meanwhile, Alissa kept messaging her that she wanted Maria to go back so that they could meet again and have some fun. Maria replied to her whenever she received her message. She received daily messages from Alissa and she gladly engaged with them until Alissa stopped messaging her. She was still on her social media accounts when suddenly Alissa vanished from all such platforms.

Chapter 13

Their sleep was disturbed terribly because the sudden knocking of the door became loud banging. Before Maria and Mikael could do anything about it, two people had broken into their hotel room. They were covered in masks while holding guns. The broken bits of light through the lamp had also fallen because they were threatening the couples with their weapons.

"Don't move!" said the person in front.

"Or we'll shoot!" said another.

Maria and Mikael were bewildered. Nothing was making sense to them. There was a peculiar dignity of plea and then despair on their faces because they knew the people in their room had a purpose. The second person had taken out some ropes. The one in the front began to tie Maria's hands behind her back. She was still in a state of shock and horror. The inexplicable expressions on her face were simply the definition of hopelessness.

"What the hell are you doing!?" exclaimed Mikael.

"Don't talk!" The man in the mask showed his gun to him.

After that, Mikael stopped talking. In the hallway, Maria was thinking about what kind of situation she was really in. Were she and her boyfriend now part of some mafia situation? Were they hostages? Nothing was making sense. There were some people in the hallway. Nobody did a damn thing about it. What on earth was going on? Mikael was just behind her. She turned back and saw that his face was drawn with so much suffering that Maria knew he was thinking the same about where they were going. They were questioning their lives: where was it headed? That was the essence of their fear and uncertainty. The terror of the situation had locked them into the present moment, but the couple didn't have any control over their lives. The heartbeat was too high. The necessity of the situation made their eyes wide. By this time, they were in the lobby. The receptionist there, who Maria recognized, just mumbled how sorry he was.

Nobody did anything. The guns were the mode of threatening Maria and Mikael. Other than that, there was no violence—but was that guaranteed? The moment they sat at the back of a car, their eyes were covered with a band. Before that happened, the couples could see that there were more armed men in the car.

"What is going on!?" asked Mikael in an audible cry of pain.

"Shut up! If you don't, someone else will!" answered one of the men.

Even though Mikael was a bit resistant to getting forcefully taken by somebody in the middle of the night, Maria was still determined. She didn't lose her composer. Yes, she was terrified. Yes, she was tense, but she wasn't sure what the cost of her decision to find her friend would be.

"Where are you taking us?" asked Maria in a voice that was neither tense nor intoned.

"Just wait," one of the men replied.

After that, no questions were asked. Both Maria and Mikael didn't want to push any buttons. The atmosphere inside the car was claustrophobic. There were strange scents that had clubbed together, making the couple feel subliminally that they were foreigners in the wrong place. Mikael's deep breaths were also audible to Maria. It was already uncomfortable. Now, with their hands tied behind their backs and eyes covered—and the fact that it didn't seem like the journey would be coming to an end soon—they were extremely nervous. It would make anybody nervous in this type of situation. Maria and Mikael weren't the exceptions. Besides, the armed men didn't say anything. Neither of them talked nor did anything so that a clue could be given as to where the couple was being taken. This strange journey of abduction was too damn long. It felt like a psychological mystery. It engulfed the minds of the abductors in so many thoughts that it felt like the fear was paddling itself. All it needed was just the mind. Yet a perception was formed of what lay ahead of the eyes. It was all blackness. The silence was more deafening. Real communication was needed.

Maria and Mikael were really afraid. The only thing they could think of was: were they being taken to the leader of some kind of mafia? What the hell was going on!? When the car suddenly stopped, that was the only clue. This terrible journey felt like an eternity. Besides, as the car stopped, the couple were forced out of the car. The manners around them had started to become rough. Yet the eyes didn't have any vision. The perception was distorted. Fear was making their minds boggle. It was already hard to get out of the car with their hands at their back. Now, to move was another struggle. Plus, the people seemed to be bad strangers with the ability to do evil things.

"Move fast!" another man yelled at them.

But the only question in Maria's mind was: how? She was trying her best. She knew by the way she was walking that Mikael was beside her. It was at that moment that they heard the sound of a metal door opening. From feeling a mild air in the atmosphere for some seconds out of the car, they were back to feeling a warmer atmosphere. The only thing that was different was the murmur of the hordes of people. Nothing was clear because they were all speaking in their native language. All this was followed by the walk on the stairs. It was quick until Maria and Mikael sat on what felt like chairs. The heartbeat was still at its zenith because someone was uncovering the blinds to bring back the vision of their eyes.

The same happened when their hands were untied. What they finally saw before their eyes was something unexpected. The essence of the whole night was as if things had started to feel secure with Mikael until something unknown had loomed and struck them. Maria then abruptly rose from her chair.

"I've been looking for you all this time," she said. "I went to so many places. I came to Side twice during the past two months. I went to Berlin to meet your parents while I made some new friends. Then my boyfriend showed up at my hotel room the day before yesterday in Palm Resort. Now I'm here. Now, I'm finally looking at you, Alissa. I wondered what happened to you."

Chapter 14

Adem didn't say much when he looked at the couple. He was more than familiar with Maria. Seeing Mikael with her was a surprise for him because he didn't know Maria had a boyfriend. He was also amazed to see how they had gotten so far. Reading Maria's expressions and witnessing the perceptible change in her posture made him think to not start the conversation by asking questions but by comforting them. "I didn't want to bring you guys like this," he said.

Maria heard his words, but in her mind, she had only one question. She did ask that question, "Where is Alissa?"

"Somewhere," he replied. "The exact location? I don't know."

"Why don't you know?" asked Maria.

"Because we broke up. Two years ago. I haven't seen her since then. I don't even know whether Alissa lives here or has gone back to her parents', in Germany." Adem replied.

Maria didn't know whether Adem was lying or telling the truth. All she cared about was where Alissa was. Still not having a concrete answer to that, she asked Adem why they had kidnapped her and Mikael. He didn't give a straight answer. He was very vague in his answers. Every answer he gave held very little information. He was portraying himself as a successful businessman. Yet in his eyes, Maria could detect that he was holding many things that he didn't want to utter.

Being polite with them, Adem also saw how the couples sometimes glanced at the guards. He thought that Maria and her boyfriend might be perceiving him the wrong way. So he gestured to his men to vacate the room. When they were gone, there was silence. Adem told them to relax. Maria wanted to tell him how they could relax when they had been kidnapped and brought here. The only tinge of relief was that the men who had kidnapped them were under Adem's control. Maria was sure he was feeling the same way because she could see some guilt on his face. But to change the topic and shift the focus to Alissa, Maria asked, "What was the reason that she broke up with you?"

"It was another man," replied Adem, looking down on the floor as if he still hadn't processed the fact that Alissa had moved on. "I never imagined she would fall for him. He used to be very well known around this area and… a very competitive man. And he always had his way with everything. He was so much older than me."

"What's his name?" asked Maria.

"Ayaz," he replied.

Suddenly, Maria could see that Adem was flung hard by so many emotions that it felt painful for him to utter his name. Yet it wasn't the name Maria was hearing for the first time. She knew Ayaz. He was a good person.

"Deniz too had mentioned his name," said Maria.

"Yes, he was the one who told me about you and him," he said, directing his gaze at Mikael, "visiting Side again. I never meant to kidnap both of you. Also, I never meant to disturb you. I heard that you were looking for me, and I thought that you just wanted to meet again. But what I did to both of you...I was wrong. I'm sorry for that. It was very important for my safety."

"Your safety?" asked Mikael.

"Yes. You see, I'm very well known around here. I can't walk in the middle of the street without protection. When you become known in places like this, the people who are starting from the bottom want to make their name off of you. They seek people like me for that. Deniz must have told you this," said Adem.

"What exactly do you do?" asked Mikael.

"I run businesses," he replied. What kind? Adem didn't give an answer to that. By this time, Maria knew what "businesses" meant. Adem was using the same term Ayaz had once used when he and Maria were talking. But the difference here was that Ayaz was carefree and felt more honest compared to Adem. Also, he wasn't fearful. Ayaz lived in the moment. He was neither desperate like Deniz nor weird like Adem. Maria thought that he wasn't a prisoner of his own opinion. He not only had a way with himself, but he also had a way with others, especially when it came to conversation. There was no wonder, thought Maria, that Alissa went with a guy like Ayaz, who might be more romantic than Adem. Before Maria could ask more questions, they heard a knock on the door.

"Let me show you my place around," said Adem.

The room they were in had no fans or any other objects. It was just dark, with one light bulb hanging from the ceiling. The essence of the room was like a storeroom until Adem let them out. They were walking in some sort of corridor that was attached to the edge of a wall. Walking ahead introduced them to a lounge. The place suddenly felt pristine. The floor was furnished, and there were blue chairs with cushions. The bar was empty. Yet the place had to offer much more than that. Ahead of the lounge was a glass window that had the reflection of a swimming pool. Adem showed the couple around, walking like a gangster with his men close behind him. In every room or hallway he took them, each place appeared bigger than the previous one. His men were everywhere. From their eyes, both Mikael and Maria could detect hostility. Plus,

Maria also saw that on the side of Adem's waist, there was a gun that he kept because his jacket was open.

Every time, different men accompanied him. Some were at their posts at different gates. It was clear that Adem was clearly a big man now, yet the credentials were still shady. Whoever Maria and Mikael were seeing before them wasn't a businessman, but rather a clear-cut mafia. Both chose to remain cordial to him and not ask too many questions after they saw what they needed to see. Perhaps that's why Adem wanted them to show indirectly who he was. After they returned to the lounge, which was located in the middle of the terrace—and was like a hub for meet and greets—Adem offered them dinner. Maria thought he wasn't asking but telling them to have dinner so that he would feel nice about it, not them. This felt strange to her. So many questions were coming inside Maria's head. The prominent one still revolved around Alissa. If Ayaz was dead, then where would she have gone? Did Adem have something to do with his death?

Pushing aside those questions that raced through her mind while eating the Turkish dinner, Maria began to think about Deniz. Even though he was a guy whose aim was to earn money by displaying his fake personality—that included his irritable smirk—she wondered what he would have told Adem about them. Adem was acting quite protective; at the same time, his tone was apologetic, while he was also indirectly showing his power. To make sense of it, Maria wondered if Deniz had exaggerated about her and Mikael when informing him that they were in Side.

During the dinner, Adem kept on talking about how everyone in the streets knew him and how he helped the prostitutes, as if he was some noble person. During this conversion, Maria almost spilt her juice when he started talking about how Ayaz was a wise man but also stupid. "He would talk to anybody and would offer his help to anybody," he said, while offering Maria a tissue dispenser.

She took the box, removed a tissue, and wiped her mouth. She pushed the used tissue into her pocket unconsciously. When the dinner was over, Adem sent his men with the couple so that they could drive them back to the hotel. This time, their hands weren't tied and their eyes weren't covered; though the car's windows were tinted. Maria and Mikael couldn't see what was outside until they reached their hotel. When the car left, the road outside Palm Resort was silent. The couple were having a hard time digesting what had just happened to them a few hours ago when they had gone to their room. It wasn't night anymore.

"I think we should go," said Mikael. "This is a dangerous place with dangerous people."

"But where is Alissa?" asked Maria.

"I can't believe you are still wondering about that question," said Mikael.

"Well, didn't you notice Adem's eyes? He still upset that Alissa left him," replied Maria. "But I guess what happened to us today… Perhaps, we should leave."

Mikael began checking the tickets while Maria went to the bathroom. After a few minutes, she came out with a stunned look on her face. Seeing Maria holding a napkin, Mikael was alarmed and asked her, "What is it?"

Maria showed him the napkin. It read, "Help me." The ink was slightly fading away.

"Oh my God," he said. "Do you think…"

"That it's Alissa? I think so, but that's not all," she turned the napkin. An address was given there. It was the name of a local town. Mikael was quick to find that place using his mobile and told Maria that the place was in the vicinity, not too far ahead. This information made the couples quite excited. But deep down, both knew they had to be fully observant, fully conscious, but devoid of any reaction to not show they were on to something now.

As it was the time just before dawn, the couple waited until a proper morning blossomed. Both couldn't sleep or rest properly, with everything that had happened to them and what they had just discovered. None of them knew what they were about to uncover when they left the hotel after having their breakfast. Maria told Mikael that they were finally going to see Alissa, but he reminded her to check her premises. Upon every major revelation that they had encountered till now, they both thought they were just one step away from finding Alissa, yet that wasn't true. Mikael ended up telling Maria to be more cautious because Adem could have his men tailing them.

Going outside the hotel, one thing that both of them had in common was fear. It wasn't that long before they were kidnapped by a man that Maria once called her friend. Even though he was acting like it was almost yesterday, Maria knew Adam didn't have good intentions. She also thought that perhaps he was the one behind the killing of Ayaz. She got that feeling when she was talking to him and slowly thought to not ask too many questions. That feeling was like an unspoken understanding. Maria was having second thoughts about it when she and her boyfriend booked a cab.

The car was going almost outside the area of Side. Meanwhile, the environment didn't feel calm. The sky seemed to have an unnatural pallor. Maria could see on Mikael's face a look of solemn stress. It did not make sense to her. Why was he so stressed now? Also, it was the look of cautious appraisal of where they were heading. The beachy landscape was changing. More country houses had started to appear, and more than twenty minutes had passed. When a cluster of new houses appeared, that was where the location was. The day was quite windy as the couple came out of the car. They looked around as the cab left to make sure no one was following them. No one was. There were alone. Among the houses, some were scattered. One of them was where the couple was headed.

The house was almost like a hut, but it wasn't shabby like Aisha's. When Mikael knocked on the door, no answer came. They stood there for some seconds. It was then Maria spoke, "Alissa? Are you there?"

Suddenly, they both heard footsteps approaching them. When the door was opened, the couple were both astonished— Maria, particularly, didn't know how to react when she saw Ayaz. "I can't believe you are alive," she said.

"You look familiar. It must have been years tho. What was your name again?", he asked.

Both Maria and Mikeal introduced themselves.

"Of course! I remember! You were here years ago, with the pretty blondes and that ridiculous optician friend, right?", Ayaz inquired.

"Yes, exactly. We heard that you have died. How can it be?", Maria was confused.

"It's a long story, please step inside, I get nervous hanging out on the street", Ayaz responded.

All three stepped inside the house. The house was clean and nicely decorated. It was neat and tidy, as if Ayaz was living there to have peace of mind. Ayaz pointed them to the living room and went to the kitchen. He returned shortly after with a very sweet mint tea.

"I was a businessman for most of my life. I was working with people, that did not always like how I did my business and wanted to take over. The people working for me are still very loyal, because I treated them right. Anyways, a few years ago, I was under constant threats. You know, power is great, until you want more and more. It can turn the best people into assholes. After many years, I was just tired of it.", Ayaz told them and exhaled.

"So, is it true that you and Alissa are together?" asked Maria.

He laughed. Maria and Mikael kept on waiting for an answer.

"You are serious? No – she could be my daughter. But I know that she was suffering. Adem was controlling, she was not allowed to do anything. I met her while doing business with Adem, and she managed to let me know, that Adem wanted me to disappear, if you know what I mean. That must have been the last time that I saw her. Shortly after, I managed to get some officials on my side, and I was officially dead. I live a life in peace now. I bought a big land for my parents, where we grow some food. It is much calmer and wonderful to spend time with my family. Together with my father, we restore some older car…".

"But what about Alissa?" interrupted Maria.

"Oh, yes, of course. She is still in Adem's grasp, I think. Adem is obsessed with her. He does not want to live without her, and he does not care about her happiness. I think she has accepted her life.

Upon listening to Ayaz, Maria showed him the napkin that read 'help me'. He raised his brow in response, especially when he saw the given location on the napkin. "Alissa knows that you both are here. One of my guys, must have given her my address. I can't be sure," he said.

"We have to help her!", Maria shouted. She stood up, she felt like she needed to move.

"Yes, calm down now, drink your tea. When are you leaving?", asked Ayaz.

"We don't know," answered Mikael.

"Well, you should, because you have to book three tickets," said Ayaz.

"Who is the third person?" asked Maria.

"Your dear friend, Alissa."

"But you just said that she is under Adem's grasp," said Maria.

"Yes, she is. Adem also thinks that I'm dead. What I'm saying is that he is stupid and impulsive. He sure is in power, but people fear him, they are not loyal. What he thinks he did to me, people who consider him a competitor want to do the same thing to him. It means that he is cautious… afraid of his death. Which means he thinks more about himself than Alissa. What I'm trying to say is that I promised Alissa that I would repay her, for the information she gave me. I think the right time has come. Give me a moment", Ayaz said, while walking out of the room.

He was now in the kitchen and talking in Turkish. Maria and Mikeal could not understand a single word. The couple was confused. Just a few seconds passed, when Ayaz reentered the room.

"Adem and Alissa will go to the prayers tomorrow. Luckily for us, the mosque Adem goes to, does not allow women. Alissa will beg him, to go to another mosque, that allows her to pray to. Hopefully, he will just believe that she changed her mind and agree. A friend of mine will wait behind the woman's entrance, to take her place, so Alissa can sneak away. One of my man will then take her to the airport.", Ayaz took a breath.

"Take this" he handed the couple a passport, "I had it made some time ago. It's for Alissa. Book a flight around noon. Take a flight that goes to Serbia, Spain or Norway somewhere closer to Germany, but not Germany. Then continue by car or by train. Adem will try to find you. You have to throw him off your trail.", Ayaz said.

Maria was impressed. Mikael turned to look at her, unsure whether to trust Ayaz or not, but she was insistent when she told her boyfriend to book the tickets right away. Mikael obliged that request and then announced in the room that three tickets had been booked for tomorrow. Ayaz nodded his head upon hearing that news. He was also quick to remind everyone that if anything went wrong, this whole plan could fall apart. Mikael still wasn't feeling right about it. In his mind, what Ayaz was saying felt like a trap. Even Ayaz could spot that look on his face, but it was Maria who trusted Ayaz because she had met him previously and at this point, had no other choice. She even thought that if she met him again, things would have been better. However, Deniz had informed her that he was dead. Now, the coins were flipped. Ayaz was smarter than anybody—and patient. If there was one person that she wanted to trust, it was Ayaz.

"Just act normally when you leave," he said. "Go about your day and, tomorrow, leave normally as if nothing has happened. If everything goes according to plan, Alissa will meet you. If not, just leave and never return here again. I will take care of it"

Maria nodded her head in agreement. However, Mikael was still reluctant, but Maria changed his mind as they walked out and headed towards their hotel. Deep inside, Maria was glad that Ayaz was alive, but that feeling had changed into a thrill the moment he told them about his plan.

Returning to the hotel, Maria and Mikael were devoid of sleep. When they returned, even the receptionist looked at them weirdly. It made them wonder whether there was someone in the room waiting for them or not. The fear of being kept captive again was still there. Even though the tickets were booked for tomorrow, time went by very slowly. The relativity of time made the couple more conscious and anxious. For Mikael, he thought coming to Side was some kind of adventure for him, but now everything felt like a misadventure. He thought he was depending on some criminal to save Alissa. But this is not the case with Maria. She knew she had to be calm, but she didn't know how. She knew she had to be tough-minded, but she didn't know what tomorrow would bring.

The couples tried to sleep, but their subterranean thoughts told them to be vigilant. They wondered if there would be any door knocks in the middle of the night. It kept them awake until the morning arrived, and they quickly booked a cab and headed for the airport. At the end of the day, they had to act normal, and that's what they did. As they got to the airport, their hearts started to pound in their chests because Alissa hadn't arrived yet. They asked a stewardess, if she could keep Alissas passport until she arrives. At first the woman was reluctant, but Mikeal casually passed her money. There again, was the behavior that confused Maria. In this moment, she was happy that a problem was cared for, that they have not thought off before.

The boarding was at 11: 30 a.m. The couple had arrived at the airport half an hour early and boarded the plane. The next fifteen minutes were spent in utter attention and hope, but nothing happened. A few minutes later, the flight crew was rushing back and forth. Everyone was in their seats and ready to take off. Maria was thinking of how she would never see Alissa again when suddenly, an announcement was made. Someone at the check-in counter had arrived late. Maria knew that the airline staff didn't allow people who came in this late to check-in, but this was happening. Maria looked at Mikael and asked: "How much money did you give her?!". Mikael shrugged his shoulders.

"All the money we had left, I didn't have time to calculate how much it was, but I guess enough?", he answered.

Everyone was wondering what was going on.

 When Alissa entered, she had an inexplicable expression on her face until she met Maria's eyes. Everything about Alissa was changed. She appeared more mature. The reflections of age could be seen on her, yet she was still beautiful. She began to cry until Maria hugged her tightly and Alissa ended up sitting beside her. Maria really heaved a big sigh of relief when it was announced that the flight was ready for take-off. She was ready to hear Alissa's side of the story. But Maria gave her time. She looked at her boyfriend. He now understood why his girlfriend trusted Ayaz so much. Maria was also quick to inform her that they were going to Spain and from there back home.

"Thank you for all that you have done," said Alissa. "I am so relived.".

"How did you escape today?" asked Maria.

"Ayaz's man was able to divert the other guards' eyes from me. From there, he took me to the airport."

Their conversation continued. Alissa still had funny ways of putting things together. Maria was also able to slip in the question about why Adem was requesting money from their parents. Alissa told her that she was with him when Adem started helping the prostitutes. He needed money for that and to organize such a business. "I thought he was standing for a good cause. I was so much in love with him that I didn't think straight. I started to become like him until I realized how he was climbing up the criminal ladder. When I told him I couldn't fool my parents and make their life miserable, he slapped me, and after that, things between us became complicated. I met Ayaz at the right time. He made me a better woman. In that process, I began thinking about whether my parents would forgive me for what I had done or not, but Adem kept me trapped for years…Kept me isolated from everyone until you guys appeared, looking for me."

Alissa went on to tell her part of the story. It made Maria realize that her efforts hadn't gone in vain. She turned to look at Mikael, who had finally fallen asleep. As far as Alissa was concerned, seeing her safe was enough for Maria. She knew and was sure that she was safe and, on her way, back to her family.